BEHIND YOU IS THE SEA

BEHIND YOU IS THE SEA

A Novel

Susan Muaddi Darraj

SWIFT PRESS

This paperback edition first published 2025
First published in Great Britain by Swift Press 2024
First published in the United States of America by HarperCollins Publishers 2024

3 5 7 9 8 6 4 2

Copyright © Susan Muaddi Darraj

The right of Susan Muaddi Darraj to be identified as the Author of this Work has been asserted in accordance with the Copyright, Designs and Patents Act 1988.

Thank you to World Literature Today and Red Hen Press for allowing us to use the words of Ibrahim Nasrallah and Lena Khalaf Tuffaha, respectively.

Designed by Ad Librum
Offset by Tetragon, London
Printed and bound in Great Britain by CPI Group (UK) Ltd, Croydon, CR0 4YY

A CIP catalogue record for this book is available from the British Library

ISBN: 9781800754195
eISBN: 9781800754188

*To my children,
Mariam, George, and Gabriel*

You have to be loyal to your exile as much as you are loyal to your homeland.
—Ibrahim Nasrallah

> if all that breaks our hearts is
> yesterday,
> and the silent colonnade
> anticipating
> the dynamite,
>
> if all we love
> is a lost world
>
> then let the dust
> swallow our names
>
> let the maps
> beneath our feet
> burn.
>
> If all we are is past,
> who are these millions
> now
> gasping for air?
>
> —Lena Khalaf Tuffaha, "Ruin"

Contents

A Child of Air *1*

Ride Along *17*

Mr. Ammar Gets Drunk at the Wedding *47*

The Hashtag *63*

Behind You Is the Sea *87*

Gyroscopes *117*

Cleaning Lentils *135*

Worry Beads *161*

Escorting the Body *203*

Acknowledgments *241*

A Child of Air

Reema Baladi

Amal calls it "the thing" too, but I hear she's getting rid of hers. Her brother is a cop and he's planning to find the money somewhere. Torrey says he's probably running drugs like the other crook cops do. Marcus isn't one of those. We all grew up together, I tell Torrey, and Marcus is solid. Torrey is trying to get me the money to get rid of it too, but here's the other thing I have to tell him: even if I had the money, I'm keeping mine.

What Torrey doesn't get . . . what nobody gets . . . is this is the best thing that's happened to me.

Torrey's not bad. It's just he's been here before, in this

situation. One girl he got into trouble was Tima, who rents a room in a house near Hopkins, and she went during week twelve, okay, week *twelve*, to take care of it. It happened with some girl from Dundalk too, he said, but she didn't want to see him so he just sent her the money, a wad of fifties, with his friend.

He doesn't want to get married or anything, and since my father is dying, it doesn't matter anyway. Amal's father is all strict, but mine is sick, and having a sick father exempts you from most Arab rules.

Here's how it is with us: usually your mom also keeps you in line, to make sure you do your duty: grow up slim and gorgeous so you can be a doctor's wife, get your nails done every week, and have a cleaning service. Amal and I both got skipped when they handed out tough moms, but not because we're lucky or anything: Amal's died a long time ago, and my own mom is like a ghost. Like when I told Mama about the thing, she just looked at me with her phantom stare, like I wasn't even standing in front of her. She spends all day either praying for Baba or scrubbing invisible stains out of the linoleum floor. A lot of times, especially lately since he's worse, I find her with her elbows propped on a pillow at the windowsill, looking down on Wolfe Street and watching everyone else live.

"Your mom is nuts," Torrey says one day, after I told him I'm thinking of keeping it and maybe she can help after it's born.

"So?" See, I don't even deny it.

"Just telling you how it is. She can't take care of herself but you want her to take care of my baby."

"No, I want her to take care of *my* baby."

"Come on, Reema. She's crazy."

"The whole block says the same thing. You think I care what they think?"

"How 'bout me?"

"Oh? You?" I say, all tough. "I don't give two fucks what *you* think."

He stares at me when I talk shit like that, and then he gets a big smile over his face and usually ends up kissing me. He does that now, and he did it when we first met too.

I was working at the Aladdin restaurant and qahwah, owned by Mr. Naguib, but everyone calls him al-Atrash because he's deaf. He's from the same village as my parents, Tel al-Hilou, and Baba used to do odd jobs for him; that's why he hired me, when he heard Baba's cancer was back with a vengeance.

It was good for me that al-Atrash couldn't hear anything because that meant I answered all the phone calls and took reservations. Torrey used to hang out at the deli next door and he'd walk by to check me out. Sometimes to wave. Sometimes he would pretend to ignore me but just stand there, posing in his tight jeans and denim jacket. I would stand at the desk by the front door, and there was a big picture of some sultan-looking dude on the wall behind me. Some ugly-as-fuck velvet picture that al-Atrash found at a yard sale in Canton.

One day, Torrey stood by the door and winked at me.

I rolled my eyes and turned my back.

The phone rang. "Why you can't even smile, girl?" he said, and I whipped around to see his face near the glass, his ear pressed to his cell phone, his grin so damn big and corny.

He'd call all the time after that. He'd sing that Groove Theory song to me that I liked, especially that line: "'You're so lovely when you're laughing,'" he'd sing in his deep voice. "'It makes my day to see you smile.'" Over and over. Sometimes he'd call and just sing it to me, that one line, watch me to make sure I smiled, then hang up. A lot of times, while we snuggled after, he'd tell me all the people he thought I looked like, and one of them was Amel Larrieux, and that made me happy because she is so beautiful.

Torrey was the first person in my life to ever tell me I was beautiful. I mean, he's mad because I'm not listening to him right now, but in some ways, he is dedicated. He called me "baby girl" even though he's only two years older than me, but because I'm still in high school, he thinks he's an adult and I'm not. If he'd known back then how I was the one dealing with Baba's sickness, with Mama being a phantom, and even with taking care of my baby sister . . . he'd know for sure I was a grown-ass adult.

The first time we went out, I lied to Mama and said I had to work late. She never talked to al-Atrash herself, she never talked to anyone really, and Baba was so sick by then anyway.

All he did was lie in bed and gasp when the pain would set in, sweating and sucking in his breath so sharp until Mama gave him the pills. Those things just knocked him out, as far as I could tell, and even though I was glad he wasn't in pain, I missed him. I felt bad lying to Mama, but it was so easy to do. Baba never let me out, but now that he didn't know me from my little sister, I figured this was what they call a silver lining. Mr. Donaldson in English class said that all the time: "If there is a silver lining to the death of Romeo and Juliet, it's that their families realize the error of their ways." Not sure about that, I remember thinking. Fuck their families, honestly.

So, that first date. Torrey walked me to the Burger King on Greenmount. I just ate small fries so he didn't think I was a heifer plus I had no clue if he was going to pay for me. How would I know? I told him I had to be home by nine—that's what time I would normally be home anyway, if I was working at Aladdin. Mama didn't ask a lot of questions, even of the home nurse who came on Fridays—she just absorbed whatever you said and didn't comment. Didn't repeat anything. When Mrs. Miranda from down the block asks me why my mom doesn't talk to her—"What, she don't like me or something?"—I tell her she doesn't even talk to *me* so don't take it personal.

"You live where?" Torrey asked me, as he bit into a Whopper. He had three lined up in front of him.

"On Wolfe," I said, delicately dipping a fry into the ketchup, trying to be cool.

"Your family?"

"What about them?"

"Got one?"

"Yeah."

"Do I gotta worry about your dad showing up here or something? I heard about you Arab girls."

I asked him if Puerto Rican fathers are any different, and he grinned and took another bite.

Sometimes in school, I can turn on a different Reema. I can be someone else when I'm taking a test. It always makes my teachers wonder if I'm somehow cheating. But it's just that I'm good at putting on a show. In that moment, with Torrey, I put on a show. I shrugged and said no like he was an idiot. And it worked. He smiled and we talked about other things: how al-Atrash is probably a racist because he doesn't like it when Torrey and his friends hang out in front of Aladdin's; how he was taking a class at a time at the community college but would probably drop it because of the money; how he was thinking about joining the military but really hated guns and the thought of killing other brown people. "I'm like Muhammad Ali, you know?" he said, laughing. "For real, though. I'm not gonna let them trick me into fighting some war, just so they can pay for classes and textbooks."

We did that, me and Torrey, a few times—eat at Burger King (he always paid) then make out in his car. He tried a lot of times before I had sex with him. I told him I never did it before, and he smiled that charming smile and promised he'd do all the work. He joked a lot like that, to make me relax. And the first time was really nice. That's why I kept going back, even though he didn't wear a condom. "I'll pull out," he promised coaxingly. "I know, baby girl . . . I know what I'm doing." And because I didn't, I stayed quiet.

He was gorgeous, I thought that even then, and his eyes were green. They stood out like emeralds in his brown face. That, plus the curly hair on top of that head? I was gone. I would have lied to Mama a thousand times just to be with him again.

And now we're here.

Now he wants me to do what Amal is doing, and he's mad because I'm being stubborn. "I have zero dollars," he says. "Nothing. And I'm not going to marry you." He doesn't say this mean, just matter-of-fact. I know he's not with anyone else, because his friends tell me how he's obsessed with me, plus he calls me constantly. He has a beeper, so if I call it, my own phone rings within seconds. He even comes to the doctor with me, because I figured out how to get checkups without Mama knowing a thing.

"This is wild," he says, looking at a poster of a growing fetus in the womb. And when the doctor hands him the stethoscope and he hears the heartbeat, he bursts into tears.

~~~~~

Baba is getting worse, the nurse says. She talks to me sometimes because she doesn't think Mama understands her.

"She understands you," I tell her, "but she doesn't know what to really say."

"He has about a week," she says, patting my shoulder with large, strong hands. "I'm going to make him as comfortable as I can."

Comfortable means pain-free, which also means he's already dead to me. He won't hear me if he's drugged up. His eyes stay open, so I surround him with books and pictures. The books are the Arabic books he likes to read, their pages thumbed and worn down so much that you can run your finger down the side and not get a paper cut. Some of them are Arabic language workbooks. He used the same books over and over when he was teaching me how to read Arabic. I wasn't allowed just to learn the dialect we spoke . . . I had to study the fus-ha Arabic, the hardcore, classical Arabic that they use only in fancy speeches and news talk shows.

He spent a long time teaching me how to read and write, how to connect the letters together because Arabic is not printed. The letters mostly slide into each other. Except for some letters—some letters, like *ra*, *alif*, and others—are complex because they don't want to be connected. They'd rather cut a word in half than reach out and link to the next letter. My name is like that—the first letter is *ra*, and it's separate from every other letter in my name. Sometimes, when Baba would make me write it over and over, I imagined that the *ra* was standing on an island, cast away from the other letters, watching as they sailed away together.

I put two small tables on either side of him and prop up pictures of me carrying Maysoon, who is two years old and has no clue what's happening. I add his wedding photo, which makes me sad because he and Mama are so young, about to board a plane from Palestine to come to America, and they look so hopeful. They have no idea what's coming.

There's one picture of when he came with me to the middle school play and someone snapped a pic of him with his arm around me. I'm in my *Nutcracker* costume—the only fairy with black hair and thick thighs and tits in a sea of skinny blonds, but I thought I looked pretty good and Baba told me that night, as he watched me onstage, that he thought I would fly.

It's a special picture because it's the only one, really. Not the only picture, I mean—the only "moment." He didn't come to my stuff a lot. He worked all the time. He worked for al-Atrash. He worked for Mr. Ammar in his strip mall, doing odd jobs: painting parking lot lines and speed bumps, cleaning the siding, installing new doors. He worked in the Thai restaurant down the block, washing dishes, making six dollars an hour. He saved some money for me to go to college, I tell Torrey, despite all this. He still saved . . . which I cannot believe. He saved it for me, and told me one day he needed me to find good work and save it for my little sister. He would help me, but I would have to help Maysoon. He couldn't do it for us both.

In English class, we're getting ready for the AP exam in May, months away. As far as I can figure, if I keep it, I won't be taking that exam at all. But I prep for it anyway. Our class is small, about fifteen kids, and Mr. Donaldson makes us practice by writing short-answer responses to specific questions. I usually do well on them because I always know to "back up what you say." If you say, "The poet has an ambivalent attitude towards death," you must back that shit up with evidence.

But today, I'm not ready. Mr. Donaldson gives us a Robert Louis Stevenson poem, "To Any Reader." I'm into it from the beginning. That's never the problem. I read really well—English and Arabic—so my comprehension is like nothing you've seen. But this poem . . . the ending is what gets me: "It is but a child of air / That lingers in the garden there."

I don't write a word. I just think of all the sadness that's suddenly in my heart. How can one line, "a child of air," do that to you? It's not what the poet meant, for sure. But I'm taking it that way. Because that's what is at stake here. I don't want to be haunted by a child of air. My mother is already made of air. My father is basically gone.

Torrey? Torrey loves me. But I know better than to depend on anyone like that.

I take a zero on the writing and avoid Mr. Donaldson's eyes.

When I walk home, I think about the craving I have inside of me. It's like an empty spot that I can never fill. I pause at the crosswalk, watching the cars zip by. Instead of crossing the street, I turn back and make a right on Mitchell, towards Amal's house. The other Arab girls at school have been talking about her. Even though she's in the same situation I'm in, I haven't talked to her in so long. It bothers me to hear what they say, because they are worse than white girls in some ways. Their dads are the type who were already doctors and lawyers when they left Palestine. Or they had money and came here and started buying up shit. Mr. Ammar is like that, a real estate type. He owns the strip mall that Aladdin's is in.

Amal and I were always friends, maybe because our dads are the type who work for their dads. When you're at the bottom, you stick together.

I know their house by the large metal frame on the side, with a grapevine snaking around the poles. When my mother was normal, and when Marcus and Amal's mother was alive, they used to pick the leaves. Every weekend in June—that's what they did. And they'd clean the leaves and dry them and flatten them in Ziplocs and put them in the freezer so we could eat fresh warak all year and not the salty stuff in the jars. Now it looks like a jungle. The leaves have not been picked and they grow wild—I can see them creeping into the neighbor's lawn, over the fence, looking for more room to stretch.

Marcus, Amal's older brother, is in front of the house, trimming the shrubs under the window with big clippers. I've always had a crush on him, honestly. He looks like the painting of Lord Byron we saw in our English textbook—slick black hair and big eyes.

"Hey, runt," he says and grins. "Long time."

"How's everyone?"

"Eh. Okay. How's your dad?"

"Same."

"Did they say—"

"Any day. They said any day."

"Hey, you have my cell, right? You call me anytime, okay? You or your mom."

I say thanks and ask about Amal, and he gets weird on me. I finally get him to crack a bit, and he tells me Amal is not living there anymore. "You know how my dad is," he says, sighing. He makes a big deal about a small twig sticking out of the shrub and he surrounds it with his clippers, then decapitates it. "He's so goddamn stubborn."

We stand there for a bit, until I say, "I mean, is she okay?"

"She's okay. It was the right thing," he says. "I don't care what anyone else thinks, you know?"

"Yeah. Me neither."

I tell him I'm going home now because I have to work at Aladdin's tonight. He jokes that he better not see me smoking narghile with the old men when he swings by. "Hey, runt," he calls out as I walk away. "You call, okay?"

"I will."

~~~

The day he dies, Baba looks skinny and surprised. When he sucks in the last breath, his mouth opens in an O, like

America has shocked him at last, and freezes there. It's like he finally understood he was never meant to win here.

We'd known it was coming. You can tell. You don't even need anyone to tell you that all you have left are just a few minutes to be together, intact, as a family. So we stood around him, me, Mama, and Maysoon. The nurse with the long gray hair asked if we should call someone else, but there is no one. She stayed in the next room, to give us privacy while we waited, but she came in whenever she heard him gasp or to put more morphine in his IV. "He can hear you," she reminded us every time before slipping away again.

Americans like to talk about everything, I know. They like to share their feelings, like purging old clothing or dumping clutter. But when you're like us, you purge nothing. You recycle or repurpose every damn thing. Nothing is clutter. And as I stand here, watching my father die before he ever really lived, all I can think about is how I'm going to use these feelings I'm having now. I need someone to love, the way I love Baba. I can't love Mama because she's a ghost, and my sister is so young that . . . well, I can love her, but she may not always want it from me. Torrey is someone I can love, but he may not always be able to give it back, either. Not with the steadiness I need.

While we wait for the doctor to come in and confirm time of death, I go out and talk to the nurse. She's sitting quietly, her hands folded in her lap, and I wonder if she's praying for us. Deep inside, I hope she is.

I need to call someone after all, I say. Two people, in fact.

First, Marcus, because he knows how to handle these things. He will come here, he will tell us what to do next, and he will tell all the other Arabs the news. Then Torrey, to tell him, with my hand on my belly, I've decided where I'm going to pour all this love that's dammed up in my heart.

~~~

I miss the AP exam. I decide I'll save the money that Baba left for Maysoon's education instead—she might use it someday. Torrey is getting more and more used to the idea that he will be a father, whether he wants to be or not. But he surprises me because he's less and less mad. Sometimes, he puts his palm on my belly and waits there, looking like a child himself.

When the baby is born, Torrey tells me I can choose the name. I tell him of course I can—it's not like he's doing me a favor. I'm going to name him after my father, I explain. I'm the daughter, but my son will have my father's name anyway.

"What's your father's name?"

"Jibril."

"What's that mean?" he asks, though I can tell he likes the way it sounds, the softness, the strength of it.

"It's Arabic for Gabriel." I write it out for him in Arabic, and I show him how the *ra* in the middle of the word doesn't get connected to the other letters. "Like my name. His name is like my name that way."

"Jibril. Gabriel. Jibril." He sounds them out, slowly, tenderly. "Oh yeah," he says, smiling. "I like it, baby girl."

"I don't care if you do."

"But, baby girl? I do."

He squeezes my hand and I accept that quietly, my heart trembling but ready.

Ride Along

Marcus Salameh

My sister is on a ride along with me, buckled up in the backseat, when she tells me about her boyfriend, Jahron. I'm turning left onto Curry Avenue because they've just called in a disturbance at the Overlook Townhouses. Domestic.

"He's sweet," Amal says, her black eyes wide in her milky face. They fill up my rearview mirror. We bring civilians along all the time, and she's technically allowed to sit up front with me, but I don't tell her that. Instead I tell her it's regulation, that she'll be safer in the back.

"Wife says husband's hitting her. There's a four-year-old

boy in the house. She says he's also been hit," comes Gerard's voice over on my radio.

"Car Four Fifty, en route. Three blocks away," I respond, then shut off my radio. "Go ahead," I tell Amal. "Your friend. Tell me about him."

"When I graduate, it'll be because of him, you know."

"Oh yeah?" I go right on Taunton Avenue and look for number 225.

"He tutored me through all my English classes. He's the one who thought history was a good major for me."

"Nice." Here I'm thinking that I was the reason she'd graduate, seeing that I'd paid most of her tuition bills the last four years.

I find the house, a two-story with a fake well on the lawn. I hate those things, especially when they have the fake bucket hanging on the side. Like anyone's going to believe this family hauls water out of the ground when, if you just look up, the electric box is sticking out of the side wall and the AC unit is tucked in by the back fence. Baba has one too, except his is even worse—it's got those plastic flowers from the dollar store planted inside with rubber dirt. A fake well that's being used as a flowerpot. For fake flowers.

Lights are on in the front window. Upstairs is dark.

"Marcus? Should I stay here?" Amal asks timidly. I hate when she says anything timidly. Makes me want to remind her who she is.

"Yeah. Keep the windows up and the doors locked." I get out and walk up the driveway, where tufts of grass grow disobediently around flat round stones like they enjoy breaking the rules. My eyes sweep around and up and down the street. Upstairs. Downstairs. It's quiet and I don't like it.

I knock three times, hard, and the front door opens. Blond with a red, puffy face. Red eyes. "It's okay. I'm okay," she mutters. Her face and chest are dotted with sunspots. They're even on her arm and the hand that holds open the screen door. The other hand is down at her side, behind her ass.

I show her the badge and tell her we received a call. "I need to see your hands, ma'am," I say, and she pulls out her hand quickly, then hides it again.

"We're really okay," she says again.

"Well, I still need to ask you some questions," I say and smile. "They make me ask, since you did call. Sorry."

She nods nervously, looking over her shoulder.

"Are your husband and child home?"

"Oh yes, we're all watching the O's game. It was just stupid, a misunderstanding . . ."

"Oh yeah? They playing the Blue Jays?" She's distracted because I hold out my badge again. "Here, look at it."

"Yeah, the Blue Jays. Listen, okay, it's fine . . ."

"You should check it out, you know. I'm driving an unmarked car. I could be anybody." I hold it out, waiting pointedly, wearing a smile.

She rolls her eyes and takes it with the other hand, the one behind her. It's quick—she grabs the badge, flips it over politely, and gives it right back, but I have a few extra seconds this time to see what I need to see. The blue bruise around the wrist, the long scratch along the forearm, the bruise above the elbow where she's been grabbed.

"Who's winning?" I ask, now that she's comfortable. "The Blue Jays?"

"Yeah, the Blue Jays," she says. "Well, thank you. Sorry you had to come out for nothing."

"So, actually, the O's are playing the Yankees tonight," I say, stepping into the doorframe. "And I'm going to need to see your son."

~~~

Later, at the station, Amal watches me book Mr. Alex Joaquin IV—and he insists that I call him "the fourth"—for second-degree assault, while his wife curses me the whole time. "He didn't do nothing!" she shrieks the whole time, telling everyone: me, my captain, the wall. "I told you."

"Your son had a bloody nose," I tell her as calmly as I can because people like this really piss me off. She shrieks again and I try to tell her quietly there are people who can help her, numbers she can call. She refuses to take the social services card I try to press into her hand.

As I drive Amal back home to her apartment, she asks me what will happen to the boy. I tell her they'll start a file, watch the family to make sure he's okay living with the mother. She looks sad, tiny in the backseat, her frizzy hair stuck to her temple like spider legs. "Hey," I say, "finish telling me about your friend."

She perks up and leans forward. "Marcus, I want you to meet him. And maybe sometime soon I can introduce him to Baba. You know, he wants to meet my family . . . he's been asking." My poor sister.

"I'd like to meet him," I say.

"Thanks, Marcus. Hey, how about you?" she asks. "You seeing anyone?"

"Nobody special."

She leans back and sighs. "You're lying," she says.

~~~~

The next day I drop off my father's groceries. Baba lives alone in the house. It's been fourteen years since my mother died. He's changed nothing, really, except to take down all the photos of Amal and hang up my picture—the one from the police academy—in the living room. It's my best photo, in the uniform. I've got my first medal on, my eyebrows and sideburns are still black. Can you believe that I used to get this paint that you comb in your hair, and you know I used it on my eyebrows. Yes, sir. If my mom were still alive, I would ask her to do it for me. I would ask Michelle, but she would just give me a weird look and accuse me of being a girl. But I'm not being a girl. It's just that it's wrong for a thirty-eight-year-old man to have white hair.

Baba comments on it every time I see him. "You getting old. You need to get married." But I ignore him every time he says it because if there is anything he hates more than Benjamin Netanyahu, it's Michelle Santangelo. Today, I walk in and set the bags on the counter and unpack: cans of chickpeas, cans of red kidney beans, bags of bread, so much bread. The man eats three bags of it a week but he's still as lean as my nightstick. Just as leathery too, because he still smokes a pack and a half a day and is always pissed because it's something I refuse to buy for him. "Wallah, I pay you back, ya kelb," he argues, but it's not the point and he knows it, and calling me a dog won't intimidate me, not the day after an abuse victim called *me* the asshole.

"You want the milk upstairs or down?" I ask.

"Down," he says from his favorite spot on the kitchen stool, where he's busy puffing away and reading the *Jerusalem Times* on his iPad, which is really my old iPad. One of his Umm Kulthum tapes plays in the old boom box, which was mine when I was in high school. "What the hell Abu Mazen is doing?" he mutters but he's not really digging for an answer, not from me, because I've never been to Palestine. We never had the money growing up, and Baba stopped talking about it after Mama died.

I head downstairs, to the second fridge. When I was a kid, my mother bought a used fridge-freezer and kept it in the basement to store extra food. My mom was a wizard shopper. "Look, ya Marcus," she'd say, pointing to the register before handing over her coupons. And the subtraction would start: "Two dollars off two, one dollar off one—but double the coupons, Marcus." And I'd watch eighty-nine dollars wither down to forty. "That's why I love this country," she'd say, and the cashier would laugh every time. She knew them all on a first-name basis, asked about their grandkids, their bad backs, their knee surgeries, told them how lovely their hair looked. "I have a lot to learn from you," one of them, a middle-aged white lady with red hair, always told her when she ripped her receipt off the printer.

That fridge was one of the hardest-working things in our little house. When Mama cooked, she cooked enough to feed all of Ramallah and Baltimore combined.

"You know, you have a whole bag of baby carrots down here!" I yell up at Baba.

"On the top shelf?" he calls down.

"Yeah."

"In the big bag?"

"Yeah."

"It's unopened?"

"Yes! They're here!"

"I know. Leave them there."

"You old bastard," I mutter and run upstairs. He's still on his stool, by the window, the morning sun shining through the two broken blinds and off his clean, bald head. He's wearing his brown cardigan, the one my mother knitted for him more than twenty Christmases ago, and it's held up all these years. He keeps his Lucky Strikes and lighter in the left pocket, his tissues and the remote control in the right. He wears leather loafers with white sport ankle socks.

"Marcus, you have work today?"

"At four. Till two."

"Too late for you, no?"

"It's fine." And then I just dive into it. "I saw Amal last night. She came with me to work."

He doesn't comment but his shoulders stiffen and he lowers his iPad.

He's not talking, which does something to me that few things can: it makes me nervous. I chased down two punks in a deserted alley once, on foot, unsure of backup, and I still wasn't as jittery as I get when Baba gets quiet. So I blabber on, like the meth addicts we haul into the station: I just can't shut up.

"She's got some kind of senior thesis project, where she has to be an eyewitness to stuff on the street," I say. He still says nothing, and I don't expect him to, so I start washing the fruit I bought before putting it away in the fridge box. "She looks good, you know. Healthy and strong. Seems like she's got a high GPA in her classes. She's graduating in two months, right in the middle of May . . ."

I pause because I hear the stool scrape the linoleum floor, his iPad tucked under his arm, but I only hear this, I don't see it because I don't want to look up from my washing and paper-toweling to witness him exit the room.

~~~

My mom's sister Nadya lives close by, but her house is bigger and fancier that Baba's. She married Walid Ammar, who owns a bunch of strip malls. He's an okay guy but he's one of those Palestinians who came to America with some money already in hand and he invested it well. He owns a piece of real estate in every corner of Baltimore. My dad says he's a good man, that he helps everyone who asks him, but even Baba admits that he is a pain in the ass to deal with. He's a guy who lectures you about staying healthy while he smokes his narghile at Aladdin's. "Drink a shot glass of olive oil every day," he tells everyone, while puffing out clouds of apple-scented smoke.

Here's another example: he always says our problems started when my mother died. "If she was alive, you all would be together still." To which I always want to say, "No shit." He thinks he's some genius who understands our problems, and when Mama was alive, he always criticized her. How she dressed, how she gave her opinion about the business, how she didn't take us to church on Sundays regularly. (And when he says "all your problems," I know he is talking about Amal, and it reminds me that I did not protect her reputation the way I should have, the way Baba refused to do.)

Walid Ammar is an ass, but there are at least two good things about him: his wife and his kids. There's Raed, who's my age and my buddy, but he also has Demetri, who's kind of a playboy, and Lamia, who's smart and really sweet. She's a lot like my aunt Nadya, the tiniest woman in the world. "You just tall for an Arab boy," she always says when I tease her, but I'm just six feet, not a giant, and the woman only comes up right above my elbow. My favorite way to annoy her is to lean my elbow on her head like it's an armrest, and then she'll swat me with whatever she's got: a spatula, a book, her open palm.

When Mama died, we started going to Aunt Nadya's for dinner every Sunday, and it felt nice to eat home-cooked meals again. When Aunt Nadya took Lamia clothes shopping for back to school, she also used to take Amal because Amal was only twelve when it happened. Later, on weekends when I would go away for National Guard training, Amal would just sleep at their house. My dad raised a stink about that too, because Demetri and Raed still lived at home so it wasn't proper. "They're my cousins," Amal would say in shock, and Baba just never got it that those days hanging out with Aunt Nadya were like a lifeline to my sister, stuck in the house with two men. She needed a mom to paint her nails and fix her hair and do the stuff women do with their daughters.

Raed never caught wind of the problem, so thank God for that. Because that would have really burned him up. And anyway, he went to college the next year, got accepted to the University of Maryland, College Park, as a transfer. He's a lawyer now, and 9/11 helped him get a big promotion in a way, because he speaks Arabic. My dad hates that about Raed. He's sure he's betraying "our people" somehow. "You, ya kelb," he said to me when I graduated from the academy. "Don't let them use you. You're Arab, first and always." But see, Baba, that's not what my birth certificate says, although I never said this to him out loud.

My mom would have said, in her soft way, "Well, Marcus, you are noos-noos, half-Arab, because of us, half-American, because you born here. It doesn't have to be a problem for you—make it something good." And she'd take a puff of her menthol cigarette, lay it back down neatly, and continue stirring the pot. "Your brain, your heart—they are two times bigger than everyone else's," she said, marketing it to me like it was a special two-for-one bonus. To my mom, America's glory was Macy's One-Day Sale. The 50-percent-off clearance bin at the Dollar Tree. Oh, say, can you see, by the dawn's early light. The city dump, where you can go to pick up fertilizer and mulch for free. Doctors' waiting rooms stocked with a coffee bar and jars of mints. That our flag was still there! Mama loved the USA. Even if you got sick and couldn't pay your bills, the hospital would not throw you out on the street—you sign a paper and, boom, free medical care. Free chemotherapy. Free radiation. And when your hair falls out, the grocery store cashiers who miss seeing you and your coupon wizardry put collection cans on their registers and raise enough money so you can buy a wig.

So yes, when Baba got worked up about his life, about never going home again, that's when Mama stepped in, ironed out the wrinkles, and we continued forward as a family. When Walid Ammar says she held us together, it's obvious, but it's also goddamned intense and so, so true. Because right now, we are coming apart like a cheap shirt in the wash.

Amal thinks campus would be a good place for my first meeting with Jahron. I tell her okay, as long as it's before four, when my shift begins, and she starts giving me directions to the campus café. I don't interrupt her, don't say that I know every inch, every nook and crevice of this campus, that we run active shooter scenarios on slow nights, that I've raced through the café in full SWAT armor, flipped over tables like barricades, sweeping rooms with my night-vision lights like a hunter.

All I say is, "Sure, by the panini stand. See you there."

He seems nice enough. Tall, good-looking guy. Built like a football player but with a soft, round face like a baby. I couldn't find any record on him.

"You must be proud of your little sister," he says, as we sit. His smile is relaxed, genuine, in his doughy face. "She's holding a three-point-seven GPA."

"Thanks to you," Amal gushes. She *gushes*. Her hand is on his arm.

"No," he says. "No, *you* absolutely did it." And he says this so firmly that I wonder if he knows everything about my sister, about the stolen prescription drugs found on her when she was sixteen. Running away, or as the cops told my dad, "moving out," when she was seventeen. The abortion she had when she really hit rock bottom. I didn't buy a class ring that year, the year I graduated from the academy, because the four hundred dollars paid for her D&C.

Does Jahron know all this stuff, the résumé of haram that would make an Arab guy squeamish and run in the other direction?

So we talk while we eat. Jahron tells me he is in graduate school here, studying—and this is where he floors me—classical music.

I honestly, totally don't know what the fuck to say to that. A grown man spending thousands of dollars to study opera and shit. So I just nod, but he catches it.

"Does that seem odd to you?" he asks in a really formal way.

"Getting a master's in music? It's your life, right?" Although I'm thinking maybe it's a good thing my sister's GPA is so high, since this dude won't be employed.

"The fine arts are always underappreciated." He sighs. "It's a modern tragedy, really."

"Sure." I say it curtly because I'm thinking how that's *not* a tragedy. Not really. A tragedy is a double homicide. Or a murder-suicide. Or a pileup on 695 when there are kids in the car. That's tragic, not listening to Mozart or Bach on some radio station that's always asking for money. "Classical music is just not what I thought, that's all."

"Is it weird because I'm Black?" he asks, and now he's testy. "You think I should be playing basketball instead?"

I stare at him, at his handsome face, long nose, large brown eyes. Amal looks like she might faint.

And I burst out laughing.

"Shit," I say, my chest heaving. "Oh, shit. You're telling me that you study classical music. And you think art is not appreciated. You know what kind of art I see at my job? My friend, I take pictures of people's brains splattered on walls. Like paintings."

"Okay, okay," he says, shaking his head. "I got you."

Amal lets out a nervous giggle, and I wish for a second, just one, that she had our mother's strength.

~~~~~

Two weeks later, I'm called back to Taunton Avenue. This time, the woman's face is busted, her nose is broken—I can tell by the funny way she's breathing through her mouth. I push past her and call out for the boy, and I find him in the kitchen, crying. He's unhurt, but I'm still pissed as I cuff the husband, who I find trying to leave through the bedroom window.

I start reciting.

". . . will be used against you . . ."

"Hey! Easy!" he shouts, his face dripping with sweat, as I twist him down on the bed.

"Shut up . . . in a court of law . . ."

"She's a bitch! She's a bitch for calling you!" he keeps yelling. "A lousy bitch!"

I finish up the Mirandas and then inform him that the child is the one who called. He can't believe it. "They teach them that in school," I tell the man. "To call 911 when they're in danger."

"But I didn't touch him!"

"Nah, you just beat the crap out of his mother, that's all."

I flip him back up, and that's when he spits in my face, a hot ball of white foam.

Motherfucker.

I rinse my face in their bathroom sink, then take him outside. "Want me to put him in?" my partner asks, smirking.

"Nah, I can do it," I start to say, my hand on the guy's neck, then slam the asshole's head into the top of the vehicle. His knees buckle. "Whoa, sorry about that. Musta been something in my eye."

After he's in, I talk to the ambulance driver. She says she's taking the mom to the Hopkins ER, but that the lady wants the boy to go to her mother's house. "She's got the address for you."

"Tell her we'll take care of it."

He's quiet the whole ride, won't say a word in the backseat. His grandmother lives over in Towson, in a quiet neighborhood, in a cute little blue house with a big porch. Before I leave him there, I crouch down and tell him he did the right thing.

"I thought he was killing her." His voice is so small.

"I'm sorry you heard that. That's pretty scary."

"I thought he was going to kill me too." And his grandmother, a gray, softer version of her daughter, rushes in and scoops him up and makes all those sweet sounds mothers make, hugs and reassurances, and I'm so thankful because these are the only things I'm never strong enough to handle on my own.

Amal gets an A on her sociology report, and she's written some flattering stuff about me. I don't understand a lot of what she's said, the terminology she's used, but I feel good at the line "Detective al-Salameh approached the house surely and helped rescue a woman and child from an abusive situation. Such everyday acts of heroism are routine aspects of a police officer's job."

Michelle comes over to my house later that night to watch the *Law and Order* marathon. "It's so nice to actually see you"—she gets sarcastic like that when I've been avoiding her. I can't help it, because she's great and all, but she wants to get married and, well, I don't. She tells people, as a joke, that she's my part-time lover, like the old Stevie Wonder song, and she knows I hate that phase of Stevie Wonder's music. And that I hate the whole fact that she talks about our relationship to everyone who's willing to listen.

She moves through the kitchen of my townhouse, her slim tanned arms reaching up to grab plates, sticking a frozen pizza in my oven, putting the beer in the freezer to cool it quickly. She moves my food out of the way to make room. "What is this?" she asks, tossing the Ziploc bag, with a thunk, on the counter. Like she owns it. That's maybe what I hate the most.

"My aunt made me extra food. Make sure you put it back." It's Nadya's garlic chicken breast, and she bagged them in batches of three pieces, enough to thaw for one dinner at a time.

"Ugh," Michelle groans.

I don't pick up on that, because I know she'll find a way to say "Maybe what you really need is a wife." Because Michelle is a great cook, and she knows it. For my birthday the last three years, since we've been together, she made me chicken marsala and I ate so much of it that I was no good in bed later. She complains about that too. But really, she's amazing, and as she checks on the frozen pizza, I realize that she's been punishing me lately in her own way, bringing over processed shit, and she hasn't cooked for me in a long time.

I don't mention this either. A few weeks ago, I did say I missed her cooking and she said I should get a service like Blue Apron, but she knows my salary and she knows I won't pay for bougie stuff like that.

I put the TV on, wipe down my coffee table—I'd been cleaning and oiling my gun on it earlier, so now I lay the gun on the kitchen counter and get some plates out of the dishwasher.

"It's about to start," I tell Michelle. She's standing by the oven, holding a dishrag as a potholder, waiting, staring at the floor.

"How long on the pizza?" I ask.

She looks up at me, pushes her black hair behind one ear, gives me that blue-eyed stare, and I know we won't be watching the first episode. I'm fucked, on my one night off all week.

She starts. Inhale. Deep, loud exhale. Voice tremor. "Got an invite yesterday to Danice's bachelorette party. They're taking her to Ocean City for a weekend."

"Yeah? You girls should have fun."

"Mark," she says. "Do you think Danice is hot?"

"What? No way," I say, and I mean it. "She's skinnier than . . . than this table leg," I add for clarity. Plus, I want to add, she's been arrested twice for DUI. There's nothing hot about someone who's always smashed.

"Do you think I'm attractive?" Tremor in the voice again. Here it comes.

"Awww. . . . Michelle . . ." I start to say.

"Do you?" She slaps the dishrag on the counter and holds her arms out, spins. "Look at me. I'm thirty-six. Am I still attractive to you?"

"You're beautiful," I say, and I mean it. She's got beautiful curves, breasts that fit right into my hands. Full lips, big eyes. I move up and try to put my arms around her waist, but she pushes me out, moves away. "What's wrong?"

"Danice's boyfriend proposes after eight months. I've been waiting on your ass for three years, Mark!" And the voice cracks, the tears fall.

"I mean, seriously, what the fuck?" she continues.

I stand there, mutely, like an idiot because I've got nothing I can say to her.

"We have fun, we like the same things, the sex is great . . ." She pauses and looks up quickly, startled. "You like having sex with me, right?"

"Hell yes," I say, and I have a moment of clarity, because I realize that having sex with her is, lately, the only thing I like about our relationship. And I feel so bad about that, like I'm some kind of creep or some jerk, but it's true.

"Then what?" And she is crying again, her voice rising. "What is it? What?"

I hear the show's opening tune, the thudding song, and know that I have already missed the setup scene. Now I'm pissed because this is how I like to relax, picking apart the actors for their crappy cop impersonations. I like saying, "They would never let him touch evidence like that," or "A judge doesn't have the right to sentence him to that." And now it's not going to happen and I'm annoyed, even though I also feel bad because I realize I've been with Michelle for at least a year longer than I should have been.

"I'm not ready to get married," I say. "We've been here. And you've broken up with me twice about it."

"But I come back."

"Yes. You do."

"I come back for you, Mark, for us!"

"Maybe you shouldn't."

That makes her gasp, and I wish I hadn't said it.

My gun is behind her on the counter, and before I can react, she scoops it up. She's handled it before, I've taken her to the range, she's even had me empty it so she could play "bad cop" during sex, but now she's so wild I feel nervous.

"Put it down," I tell her. "I don't think the safety is on."

"You care more about this," she waves it around, "than me. Right now, you're pissed that you're not watching your stupid show."

"Seriously. I was cleaning it and the safety might not be on."

"Admit it. You're pissed."

"Michelle, stop goddamn waving that gun . . ."

And it goes off, like it has to. Twice. The first bullet misses me, but plants itself into my kitchen wall, drilling a neat hole right through the drywall and into a stud.

I know—I'm sure—she let out the second one by accident, because the sound of the first one surprised her. That's what civilians don't realize—the noise and the kickback can make you lose control. That one hits the other wall, near the fridge, but not before it scrapes a sliver out of my left arm.

"Put it down!" I scream. And she listens. The blood drips out of the long, snakelike wound, and the pain sets in real quick, real bad. "Get out."

She starts to cry, and I repeat quietly, "Get out of my house."

"I'm sorry," she weeps.

The oven dings.

"Leave right now."

She is still crying as I pick up the phone and call Raed to come and help me.

~~~~~

On the way home from the ER, when my arm is stitched up, Raed buys me Taco Bell. "I told you that girl was nuts."

That's real nice, coming from Raed, the one who introduced me to her in the first place. Three years ago, when I got promoted to detective, he took me out to a classy jazz club, even though we both know shit about jazz. All we know about high class is the basic formula: more money means better quality. In that way we learned from Demetri, his older brother, who always has a woman on each arm. Even after he got married, he's still in the clubs, chilling and flirting and spending money like crazy. He brings a new woman to Aladdin's every month and shows her off, like he dares us to tell his wife. Nobody likes his wife, and not too many people like him either. But he's my older cousin and Raed's big brother so we do try to be like him, except we're maybe not as smooth. We're chasing "class" and desperate for it.

Raed told me that night, as we ordered drinks, because we knew how to do at least that, that he took a class at the community college about wine. "Because all the partners and the other associates order it like they know what they're talking about. The whole sniffing and sampling, and swirling it in your glass—it's an art form," he said. "And I don't know what I'm doing. I can't play the game, dude. I'm ordering it like 'pee-nut gree-gio.'"

"Well, how do you say it?"

"It's pinot grigio," he said in a fancy, Frenchy way.

"Fuck you," I said, laughing. I didn't tell him I think it's actually Italian, because he's supposed to be the smart one in the family and I know my role.

"It was pathetic, man, but now I paid my two hundred twenty-five dollars and got my crash course in wine. The teacher was this old man. Dude kept swirling his glass, making us swirl ours. 'Sniff it!' he kept saying. 'So crisp! So vibrant!'" And he and I were rolling, and I was imagining my dad, watching some old guy fawning over a glass of wine and scowling. My dad, who fills a shot glass with olive oil every morning and takes it straight. My dad, who claims Umm Kulthum should only be listened to when you're holding a cigarette and a glass of arak. Who used to sell bottles of J&B in brown bags in his store and curse in Arabic at the people who bought them. "Ya kelb ya sakran," he would say, calling them drunk dogs. "That mean, in my country, have a good day and god bless you."

I'd been mad that night at my dad. He hadn't come to the ceremony, hadn't called to congratulate me on my promotion. My sister was just starting at the college, in her second semester, and I didn't tell her about the ceremony because she was still going to therapy sessions at night. Raed, who'd attended with his mom, had asked where my dad was.

"He's not coming. You know he hates that I'm a cop."

"Maybe he wants you to be a gas station attendant, like we were in high school," he joked, trying to make me feel better. And that's why, after Nadya went home, my cousin and I went to that jazz club, so he could cheer me up, the way he'd been cheering me up since my mother died. "There's a really hot waitress there I want you to see. Best ass in Baltimore."

The place was an oval-shaped room, dark and lit with blue lights, domed ceiling. The bar, where we sat, was like a throne at the front of the room. Candles on every table. The band at the other end, doing some improv stuff on the trumpet.

The trumpet is the most outrageous of all instruments. In your face. Such a diva. Give me a cello, big and sad, any day.

I was just telling Raed that, with my bonus from the promotion, I was thinking of putting a down payment on a house—this house, actually—a small house in the city, because as a cop I had to keep a city address. But I'd have a small lawn and a backyard, and I was going to get a grill.

Then the waitress interrupted us.

"Need a table, Ray?" she asked my cousin.

I couldn't even respond because my breath had stopped somewhere in my chest. All breasts and legs—that's all I saw, I swear to god, but when I actually looked at her face, I liked that even more. No fake tan, no striped hair, no big earrings. I think all she wore on her face was ChapStick. Michelle doesn't need a whole lot.

"Yeah, sure," my cousin said, grinning like a wolf, and introduced us.

I flirted with her all night and Raed encouraged it. And when I left a tip, a twenty-dollar bill, she took it and, winking at me, she rolled it up and slid it into her bra. Just slipped it right between her tits. And then she took out her pen and wrote her phone number on my forearm.

"She's brazen," Raed said over and over. "Way too out there, right?"

"Fuck you," I said, thrilled.

"Just saying," he said, and suddenly looked worried.

But he's been saying, for three years now, that Michelle is fun but she's not the kind of girl you settle with. And I hated that mentality, the old Arab way of sizing up a girl based on nothing and judging her future.

That's what ruined my sister, that way of saying, "Nice girls don't do this or that."

But Raed had a point. I hate it that Michelle had to go and shoot me, which only makes his case stronger.

"She's a nutjob, cuz," Raed says now.

"She's not. She just thought, you know, that I would propose to her one day soon."

"Just move on. Don't worry about it." He talks about the girl he's dating now, Ellen, who has a cat obsession and "doesn't really have a job or anything, but she's very demure and nice."

"Demure?"

"Yeah. She's demure. That's what I said. And she has a friend who's—"

"No, thanks. I don't need a demure girl. Get out of here with that shit."

He changes the subject and tells me that his mom wants to know if anyone is throwing a graduation party for Amal.

"I never even thought about it," I admit, all panicked now, as we head outside. How could I not have thought to throw my sister some kind of a party?

"She said she'll do it, at our house, whether your dad comes or not."

I thank him and say Amal might want to bring her new boyfriend. As we clean up our taco wrappers, I tell him a little about Jahron, and his classical music degree, and how he seems good for my sister.

As the car starts up, he puts in a CD and a Billy Joel tune pours out of his speakers. "Uptown Girl," full blast, and I give him a funny look. He tells me to shut up.

~~~~

Baba comes to my house to help me patch up the hole in the kitchen wall. He parks his old silver Buick, which is longer than the actual parking space, and it shudders and moans before it actually shuts off. He comes in, carrying a bucket of spackle, and inspects the wall.

"You need a wife," he proclaims solemnly, as he pastes white mud over the hole. "But not this girl." Funny how he and Michelle both agree on this one thing: except Michelle thinks my dad is an old-fashioned misogynist and my dad thinks Michelle is a slut. He has seen her exactly twice in three years, but he waited until the second time to issue his official disapproval. "She is bretty, yes, but she will not be a good mother of your children." I think now about his words, and how I'd hated him, and everyone, for that sentiment. But now I think I knew this all along, because I'd picked up the phone when Michelle called this morning and told her it was over. She'd been stony silent the whole time, and I kept apologizing. Finally, she said, "You bastard. You've wasted my life," and she hung up.

"We broke up," I tell him. "I'm sure you're happy."

"Of course I'm happy," he says, giving me a funny look. "She shot you."

I run my good hand over the gauze, thinking how unfair he is, how unfair I have been too, to Michelle.

Baba interrupts my thoughts, tells me in Arabic, "Having a nice life with a good woman is the best thing you can hope for in this world. She will make all your days good ones."

I look at him, astonished. The old man is so blunt but he turns into a goddamned poet or something when he talks in Arabic.

Then he adds, "Until she leaves."

~~~

We finish the wall, wait a few hours, sand it down (I can only use my good arm, so he's three times faster than me), paint it over. While we're waiting, I pour him some cereal, which he refuses, then I warm up the chicken from the freezer. He bites into it hesitantly, then, deciding he likes it, he digs in. As we eat, I tell him about Amal. She's graduating, has worked hard. Aunt Nadya is throwing her a small party and it would be nice if he came to it. It was time to let go of the past. Amal is making a new start to her life and he should support her. There's even a special reception on campus for history majors. It would be a good time to reconcile. Mom would want that.

I've been building up to tell him about Jahron, but he drops it himself, like a bomb. "Is true that she dating a Black guy?"

"His name is Jahron," I say, feeling exposed, betrayed, like I'm covering a scene without my weapon. "He's a graduate student."

"He Black?"

I ignore it, try again. "He plays violin, and he's been practicing 'Enta Omri' to play for you. You know, that part where the violins come in all strong. He says the writer for Umm Kulthum was influenced by . . ."

"I don't come to America so my daughter can sleep with no Black men," he says, and he stands up. He dumps the rest of his chicken into the trash, puts the plate in the sink, slips on his jacket, inspects the drying paint one more time, and leaves.

Suddenly, I want to grab that gun and shoot another hundred bullets into the wall, bring the whole thing crashing down on all of us—me, Amal, Dad, Raed, Demetri and all his girlfriends, Nadya, even Walid Ammar and his stupid strip malls. Just topple it all and crush us under the rubble.

～～～

Jahron stands beside me at the history major reception, holding Amal's purse and cell phone. She's outside the room with the other graduates, in her blue gown and cap, the gold tassel bobbing in her face. They're waiting to file in and we, their friends and family, are waiting to applaud them.

She spots me and Jahron, waves, looks around us, and sees no one else. Her face falls for a second, and I feel a sharp pain in my chest. In the crook of my good arm, I'm holding a bouquet of two dozen roses for her, one from me and one from Mom. I'm glad I never mentioned the idea of a party to her, because Aunt Nadya called me later the same day Baba left my house. "Listen, Marcus," she said in her quiet voice, "I just don't want to get between anything here. I didn't know about her boyfriend, and if she wants to bring him, I don't want anyone to say I helped her against her father's wishes." She wanted me to say it's okay that she's not doing a party after all, to agree with her that it's too complicated, but all I said was "Okay, whatever," and we hung up being not-okay with each other for the first time ever.

"You look sharp," Jahron tells me.

"I try to clean up sometimes," I respond. I own two suits, a black one for weddings and funerals, and this gray one for happy occasions.

When Amal files in, Jahron and I clap and hoot loudly, to make up for all the others who are not there: our mother, our aunt and uncle, our father, who called this morning to warn me. The old man gave me a goddamn ultimatum: if I encouraged Amal's relationship, he would never speak to me again either. "I lost a daughter already," he told me sternly. "If I need to lose a son, I can."

But here's the thing: he's not here to see her flip her tassel from left to right. Or see her name printed in the program with an asterisk next to it (magna cum laude), watch her get the history department student achievement award for something they call the "best nontraditional student." Amal walks across the stage like a champ, shakes the dean's hand and all. And Jahron is here with us, holding her big, chunky purse. He snaps a picture of me and her, and she's clutching the roses, real flowers, smiling so big and wide that I want to keep her there always, under my arm, both of us lost together.

Mr. Ammar Gets Drunk at the Wedding

Walid Ammar

There was a man in the ballroom of the Sheraton wearing a skirt.

Mr. Ammar watched the man approach the buffet. He still couldn't believe he was at a wedding where you had to stand in line and fetch your own food. Even worse, such a shameful thing was actually the wedding of his son Raed. Everyone was sick of him saying it, but really, so many things were wrong.

A daughter-in-law who couldn't pronounce her new husband's name. "His name is Raed," he'd told the idiot a few times, but she'd laughed and insisted, "Oh, I like calling him Ray." It burned him up! *Raed* meant "pioneer," he who blazes a path—that was his son, so smart and capable and clever. He had rejected the family business and left it to his brother, Demetri. Instead, he'd gone into law, and now he made a quarter million a year. Why would she reduce that name when he and Nadya had chosen it so carefully?

What else was wrong? Nadya had asked him wearily just this morning, as they got dressed. A wedding that cost a year's salary, he'd retorted. A DJ who played American music that sounded like a video game. Most of all, a celebration less than forty days after they'd buried his mother. The mass for her soul hadn't even been said, and here was her grandson, dancing a strange dance with his skinny wife, flapping their arms like terrified birds. His new daughter-in-law who had a white cat she loved so much that it was a guest at the wedding. It sat up on the head table on a white satin pillow, presiding over the party like a princess.

And now, this man.

This man with a red beard and bare legs, at his son's wedding, eating pork on a stick istaghfurallah.

Raed didn't care about his opinion. He'd worked so hard to put him through college, to buy him a nice car, to buy him nice suits for his job interviews. And now that the boy was a man, he didn't want his father's advice. What was so bad about having some Arabic music at the wedding, he'd asked his son, in a private moment when the idiot was not around them.

"Ellen's family is proud of their culture, just like we are," Raed had argued. "You have to respect that."

But we have a culture too, he'd told Raed. "Your brother, Demetri . . . your sister, Lamia . . . both had Arabic music at their wedding. Why not you? I want to dance at your wedding." That's when his future daughter-in-law walked over and revealed she'd been listening to them the whole time. "My aunt is a harpist and she's playing a special song," she said firmly, her blue eyes staring boldly at Mr. Ammar. It was funny how she broke her own performance of sweetness to get her way in this.

Mr. Ammar wasn't stupid. He'd been in America for thirty years. He knew the elusiveness of delicate white women, how they drew Arab boys to them like planets to a fiery star, how they turned their young men into blushing, stammering fools. He saw how Ellen, with her pink nails, her slim wrists, her tiny waist, transformed Raed, his football-playing, lawyer son, his second son—a child he'd poured all his energy and love into, the child he'd prayed for—well, no matter about all that now because, like a witch, she'd changed him from a pathfinder into a mule that lowers itself to the ground for its back to be loaded. And while she was controlling him with her glossy smiles, her heavily lined eyes making her look like some kind of elf, she'd joke, "Ray and I share a culture—we're both Leos," like it was such a big fucking deal. One-twelfth of the world are Leos, Mr. Ammar wanted to shout at her every time she said it.

All around him, people talked lightly, and laughed. My mother is dead, he wanted to shout. Stop clinking your glasses. But they continued talking about the tall, dark, handsome groom and the bride who looked like a model. The man in the skirt was back in the buffet line, piling his plate with chicken, steak, and pork—so much meat, these Americans, and then they wonder why they're always so tired. Mr. Ammar thought Raed should count him as four guests, not one.

His wife, Nadya, approached, looking angelic in a silvery blue dress, even though he knew she was still upset. You'll be overdressed, he'd warned her. They'll all be wearing jeans probably. She didn't care. I'm the mother of the groom, she'd said, and I raised a magnificent son, and I'm going to look as proud as I feel.

"Are you going to eat?" his wife asked, slipping her hand into his as he strolled to the bar and ordered another drink. It felt nice to speak to someone in Arabic. Their other Arab guests fluttered around, chatting politely but looking as out of place as they probably felt. Of course they did. Nothing was familiar—not the food, not the drinks, not the music. And one of the guests of honor was a cat, who garnered more respect than the father of the groom. The dance floor—he'd groaned when he'd walked in and seen it—what kind of Arab wedding had such a tiny dance floor? In an Arab wedding, every inch of the room became a dance floor.

"You still look angry," Nadya warned him quietly.

"Why aren't *you* angry?" he asked her.

"You need to eat," she replied, wearing her patient smile. She indulged him a lot and he was grateful to her.

"This whole thing . . . everything so rushed."

"They had to marry before Lent," his wife said calmly. "You know that. It was bad timing about your mother."

"By the way," he said, shaking his head. "There is a man here wearing a dress."

"Allah yerhamha," she said. "I miss your mother too."

"They should have waited. It's not even been forty days."

"No weddings during Lent." That was the voice she used when she was annoyed with him, and it was his signal to stop. Sometimes he wanted her to drop the serene veil she always wore. For her to be as angry as he was.

"The living," he continued, "used to pause for the dead. Out of respect."

"Let me fix you a plate. You should eat something. How many drinks have you had?"

"I'm not eating." Something caught his attention. "Look . . . There he is. Do you see him?"

She ignored his question. "People are watching."

"Do you see what that man is doing?"

She finally turned and looked. "I saw him. He's very nice. His wife is the aunt. The harpist. We haven't met her yet."

"Why do we have to have *their* music but not *our* music?" Mr. Ammar asked.

"Everyone can tell that you're not happy."

"I'm *not* happy. You can see the bride's tits right down the front of her damn dress. I'm scared to stand next to her in case something falls out—"

"*Khalas.*" Her voice was firm, so he snapped his mouth shut. She put her arm through his. "I'm going to fix you a plate. And then we're going to chat with Raed and maybe take some pictures. And *then* we're going to smile and shake hands with everyone. We will mingle. You will look happy."

"There's nobody here whose hand I want to shake."

"Your nephew Marcus came. We should say hello to him. I'm glad he did, even though you wouldn't let me invite his sister."

"Her own father doesn't talk to her. Why would I invite her?"

Nadya muttered, "Allah give me patience," dropped his arm, and headed towards the buffet line. As he watched her walk away, he noticed Ellen's father approaching. Raed's father-in-law. It was too late to escape, so he drained his glass of Grey Goose as the man trudged towards him. His hair was white and stuck out at all angles on his head, and his glasses slipped down his bulbous nose. He looked like a white Husni from the Ghawar movies—a man nobody could take seriously, no matter how dressed up he got.

"I think they need us at the front for more photos, Wah-leed."

"Okay. Okay. I go get my wife."

"Just the fathers now, I think." He clapped Mr. Ammar on the back and pulled him towards the head table, where Raed and Ellen stood. "Enjoying yourself?"

"Yes."

"It's okay that we had alcohol, right?"

"Yes, of course." He held up his own glass. "I tell you before, we are Christians, not Muslims." As if to make a point, he beckoned to a waiter, handed over his empty glass, and took a fresh one off the tray.

"Gotta always ask, you know. This way the culture doesn't become a problem." He was only half-listening to Mr. Ammar anyway, waving at other guests. Before they reached the front of the room, the man stopped and waved his hand around. "Like some of your guests here, they're wearing head scarves. That's not gonna be something Ray surprises my Ellen with, right? In a few years?"

"We are not Muslims." Mr. Ammar's head started to hurt. "These are our friends."

"Right."

"But our guests—they are not forced to wear." He nodded towards Dr. Hamdi, who stood to the side with her husband. "That lady right there—she is pediatrician. She run the whole clinic at Bayview. Their daughter—she is soccer player. She play for big Maryland team."

"She wears that thing while she plays?"

"Yes."

"Some things are okay. Some things . . . I gotta ask." Ellen's father shrugged. "This country is changing. You're a hardworking man and honest. You made it big here in the States, but not all the new people coming in are like you, you know."

Mr. Ammar thought about his mother, who was so kind

and sweet and would have still looked at this man and muttered, "Kalb ibn kalb."

He glanced up at his son Raed, who stood tall beside his elf-wife and wondered, How could he do this to me?

They took the damn picture. The mothers came too. There were more pictures. He drank another glass, but saw his wife's glare and declined the next one. More and more people joined the picture—Raed's and Ellen's co-workers, cousins, friends. He wondered who would see this picture in ten years, twenty years. Maybe his grandchildren? In forty years, his great-grandchildren? He wanted them to see him smiling, but not too broadly. He was going to lose his son. He'd already lost him. And if his grandchildren grew up feeling lost in the world, unattached to anything, he wanted them to know that, even before their birth, he had anticipated this, and he had been sad.

"I wish Sitti Fayrouz were here," Raed told him somberly, as they posed for a father-son picture.

"Awww . . . your grandmother?" his tiny wife asked.

Raed nodded sadly, and everyone made a sympathetic sound, like a rush of emotion, even though they had been dancing something called a cupid shuffle a few minutes before.

He wished his son hadn't said that.

Because now he was sinking into his memory of those final days in the hospice, when she was gasping for breath. He'd sat many long hours in that room with her, just the two of them sheltering from the rest of the world. Over the beeping of her machines, she'd mumbled to him, thinking he was his dead brother, and spoke to him so lovingly in her delirium. "I missed you, Michel. Where have you been?" And in his own desperation to comfort her, he'd lied. He'd pretended to be Michel, who could make everyone smile just by walking into a room and who should have been the one to live. If the cancer was going to take anyone, it shouldn't have been Michel.

And that's why, now, Mr. Ammar couldn't stop himself from replying to his son, "You should have respected her memory, then."

"Stop, Baba," Raed said firmly.

"You're disrespecting her memory. And I don't even know why I came for this."

"Walid." Nadya.

"I'm telling you all," he shouted in Arabic, "that I don't even know why I am here. There is nothing for me at this wedding."

Several people tried to calm him. His son Demetri, the one who was always smiling and flirting with women, moved towards him. His daughter, Lamia, had been standing there, quiet as always, but moved away, maybe in embarrassment. Everything embarrassed that one.

Then he heard "Uncle Walid." That was his nephew, Marcus, who barely talked to them anymore. "Let's take this somewhere else, Uncle."

"Why are you always bossing people around?" he asked Marcus, who gave him a dry look like he wanted to pick him up and throw him. He could too, the beast—he was taller than Raed and even wider and more muscular.

"This isn't the time."

"I guess we should be glad you're even here," Mr. Ammar shouted. "How lucky for us you decided to come!"

"I'll give you one warning."

"Or what? One warning? For what?"

"Hey, come on," Demetri said, trying to push them apart. "Come on, please. This is my brother's wedding."

Raed whispered something hurriedly to his fairy wife, who walked away with her father, clutching his arm as if she couldn't stand on her own skinny legs. She hurried to the front table and picked up her cat, hugging it like it would console her.

Raed took his arm and whispered angrily in Arabic, "Are you drunk?"

"Yes," replied Mr. Ammar. "I am as drunk as Peter at the Last Supper." He yelled towards Raed's father-in-law. "Peter, you hear? Not Mohammad! Peter!"

Marcus rolled his eyes. "You're embarrassing everyone, Uncle."

Mr. Ammar felt a fury ripple through him. This beast dared to correct him, after everything he'd done for them when his mother died? "Ah, you want to open your mouth, eh? You're just mad at us because we don't talk to your sister? Isn't that it?"

Marcus became very quiet.

"Well, guess what? Nobody talks to her." Mr. Ammar had

him now. What could his nephew say to that? "Why would we? She's not welcome here. She's shacking up with her boyfriend . . ." he shouted, getting close to Marcus.

The punch hit him in the stomach, swift and fierce like a rifle butt. Later, his wife would say at least Marcus had spared him his face. People gasped and Mr. Ammar struggled to breathe for a few seconds, because of both the pain that bloomed in his belly and the fact that Marcus had knocked him flat on his ass. Raed and Demetri shouted at Marcus to get out, and from his view on the floor, Mr. Ammar watched his thick, wide back retreating, pushing through the stampede of people to the front of the hall. Some lifted him, others squawked nervously like chickens. "What happened?" "Why did the big guy hit the groom's father?" "Should we call the police?"

"No bolice. No bolice," he heard his wife imploring someone. "Everything eez okay."

"We're okay, everybody," Raed said. "Not a fight. Just an accident. My father tripped."

The muttering changed as people who had not really seen the punch began to absorb and repeat the new story.

And that was it. Marcus, who was heading out the door, was no longer the aggressor. The story morphed quickly: he, Mr. Ammar, was a drunken fool who'd embarrassed himself at his son's wedding.

"I'm leaving," he announced, standing up. "This is not right. This hasn't been right from the beginning." He walked out slowly, his hand pressed to his side. It hurt to inhale, but he raised his head high, his eyes meeting those of others directly until they looked away.

Raed didn't follow him out.

When he turned back to look, he saw Raed at the front, looking angry and disappointed, his arm around his wife, consoling her while she consoled her fat cat.

His wife and a few others did follow. "I'm fine," he told them dismissively after a few minutes, because nobody was saying how bad Marcus was, or how arrogant or wrong he'd been. He felt that they blamed him, at least partially. Eventually they wandered off, including Nadya, who muttered, "I'm going to check on Raed." Alone, he trudged through the Sheraton's carpeted hallways until he found himself in an empty lounge room. He stood under a large chandelier, assembled from thousands of glass beads, each one reflecting the light to look bigger and more important than it really was. The chandelier cascaded down into a cone, like a big light ready to beam him up to heaven. Maybe that wasn't where he'd end up, he thought, looking around at the ornate room, lined with tall vases of flowers, plush carpeting, rich sofas and chairs. He slumped onto one couch and stared up at that chandelier, which seemed to be pointed down, cocked, and aimed right at his heart.

A few seconds later, the music. It had been there the whole time, but he hadn't quite heard it until now, in his stillness. The sound rippled softly, like a qanun, through the room. He looked around the lounge—he was alone, but he realized it was coming from a side room. Standing up, he lurched unsteadily towards what looked like a break room for employees. Inside, servers in black vests and pants stood listening reverently to a woman hugging a large harp as if it were a child.

He didn't recognize the song she was playing and humming, but it soothed him. And then she looked up, stared into his eyes, and he gasped loudly.

"You," he said, holding out his hand.

"Hello," she said quietly, tilting her head to the side just as she used to do before. "What a coincidence."

"My God. I thought I will never see you again."

"I do see patients' families sometimes. How lovely to reconnect." She stood up and took his hand, pressing it warmly between both of hers. He remembered that too, how she'd cradled his hand like a prayer. "We did go through a lot together that week, didn't we?"

He remembered how warm her hands had felt rubbing his back, holding the beads on his rosary for him when he'd collapsed into sobs. They were not smooth hands, but supple like broken, worn leather. They'd lifted his mother by the arms, these hands, held a stethoscope to her chest, and then her back. They'd dipped a sponge into a shallow bucket to clean his mother's legs and feet, and they'd run a comb through his mother's long, uncut white hair. And in the end, in a final act of grace, these strong hands had pulled the sheet over his mother's contorted, twisted face.

"The groom is my son."

"Ah. The bride is my niece. My husband's niece, technically. I promised her I'd play for her. It's an old family song."

"Your husband . . . he's out there?"

"Yes. Did you meet him? He has a long beard."

"The man wearing a skirt?"

She laughed softly. "I always remember our conversations so fondly." She was indulging him, he could tell, the way his wife did. "It's called a kilt. I'm sure you've seen one before. Our family tartan is the design he's wearing."

It's still a skirt, he wanted to say, but he kept the thought in his own mind. There suddenly didn't seem to be any pleasure in packing his opinions into a bullet and firing it into his listener. He believed, so strongly right now, that he would rather hurt himself than insult this woman.

"Thank you for what you did. For my mother."

"It was a blessing to know her, even for a few weeks. She was lovely."

He squeezed her hand again, his throat thick, but his mind clear.

"Will you come and listen to me play?"

"Everyone in there." He shrugged. "Nobody happy with me."

"Oh, I can't believe that."

"It's true."

"I'd love for you to hear the song, though." She patted his shoulder. "Won't you come and listen?"

He did, sitting just inside the door at a vacant table, as she fluttered her hands over the strings, pulling out a lovely, echoing sound, and complementing it with her pretty voice.

He'd walked in on her once singing to his mother, he remembered: the "Ave Maria." Nadya's head was craned, looking around the room for him. She was always making sure he was safe. I'm back here, he wanted to tell her. I'm okay. I'm listening.

The Hashtag

Rania Mahfouz

She'd glimpsed the hashtag on her Twitter feed that Tuesday morning. She saw it again later in the afternoon on Instagram. #Justice4Rasha. She didn't know what it meant or who Rasha was or why she needed justice, although she did wonder why many of her friends were retweeting it. But she couldn't give it her full attention, because that morning, she had a problem.

Not a problem. If Rania was honest, it was a crisis. And she was handling it alone, as usual, without Yousef.

When the email arrived that morning, things had already been hectic. Yousef had come home the night before from his trip to Palestine. She'd picked him up at the airport Monday night and driven home in silence, knowing her little vacation away from his moods was over. And when he'd gotten up and gone to work, and when Eddie had been packed off to school with his lunch and books, she'd made coffee and sat down to breathe.

That was when she'd scanned Twitter briefly and seen #JusticeforRasha. But then she'd checked her email and read the devastating message from the principal. The stupid school was trying it *again*—working against her, not with her. But this time, they weren't moving Eddie to another class, or taking away his class aide. This time, the threat was to hold him back another year. Fighting a public school system was like standing at the edge of the ocean, she thought; you're determined to hold your ground, but it will drag you in until you're up to your knees in salty water. The icy waves will crash against you, tempting you to flee and go somewhere safer, warmer. They will make it hard for you to stay.

For years, she'd been handling paperwork—teacher evaluations, medical diagnoses, the forms that were numbers and letters, 504, IEP. It was all draining her, and that morning, with the new threat, she'd had to face facts.

She needed an advocate.

So, on that Tuesday morning, she wasn't worried about Twitter. Instead, she was on the phone, calling lawyers, asking about rates, and checking past threads on her ADA parenting Facebook group. That group had saved her since the diagnosis three years earlier: the other parents there had coached Rania on getting Eddie tested, on the differences between dyslexia and dysgraphia, how to explain Asperger's to laypeople. She especially learned how to approach teachers and principals. Sometimes she would log off Facebook and watch Eddie at his plastic table, or lying on the floor, coloring or pushing his trains, and she would wonder how her beautiful boy could have been served up such a menu of challenges. Then she'd remind herself that he needed a mother who was also a warrior.

Yousef was not a member of their army. He'd designated this battlefield to her command. Instead, he was a monarch who shrugged over the victories and blamed her for the losses. She waited until he came home from work on Tuesday evening to tell him the news. He'd snapped, of course. "They can't hold him back again. Do they want him to be fucking twenty-five by the time he finishes high school?"

I am at the edge of the water, she thought, and my toes are wet and cold, and my heels are sinking in the sand. She calmed her voice before answering.

"There's a meeting Friday before school," she explained, watching as he emptied his suitcase. "If we show up together—"

"I've been away for two weeks. Do you know how much I have to deal with at work right now? You deal with this. Jesus." He flung his clothes into the laundry basket.

She'd backed off, trying to understand. Two weeks ago, he'd gotten the call from Palestine. His mother was ill, so he'd flown out the next day. She'd recovered almost miraculously during his stay, but yes, he was exhausted. Trips back home drained you—she knew that. He visited elderly relatives, helped others with their legal issues, and even attended his young cousin's funeral in Ramallah.

Destiny put everyone on a stage, to play a role, and sometimes the spotlight slipped off you to give you a break. At other times, it burned into you directly, relentlessly, as you stumbled through a soliloquy of exhaustion. She'd experienced this before: she'd been a warrior when her father's cancer had almost killed him and again, two years later, when her mother's heart had nearly stopped. She'd managed the doctors, the driving, the medications; she could give an injection as smoothly as any nurse and could handle radiation drugs like a specialist. "You're our rock," everyone told her, but that reputation didn't feel like a compliment anymore. It felt like neglect. She was juggling so much with Eddie, and nobody said, Rania, let's go out to lunch. Rania, talk to me about your feelings. Rania, sit here, habibti, and rest.

All this ran through her mind on that day the hashtag came through. At one point, her cousin in San Francisco texted her—"Have you seen the hashtag?"—but Rania ignored it because she was on a Zoom call with Samira Awadah, Esquire, who had fourteen years of experience in the public school system and whose name she had picked out of the list because it was an Arab one.

"The families I represent don't get sidelined by the system," the lawyer explained in a crisp, husky voice. Rania could imagine her in a courtroom, wearing those thick, black-rimmed glasses, staring down a judge, and daring him not to vote in her favor. Then again, she probably rarely was in court. Rania knew from her group that an advocate's days were spent in principals' offices across the city, arguing with teachers and administrators.

"I have a friend, Johnnie Davas's mother—she's in my ADA advocate group," Rania told the lawyer. "She said you really helped her with their situation."

"I can't talk specifics about other children and families."

"Oh! Of course . . . I wasn't asking."

"Or even acknowledge it."

"I'm not. I wasn't trying to . . . I mean—"

"You weren't asking me to divulge information."

"Right." Rania hesitated. "My English is not always the best. Do you speak Arabic, by any chance?"

"I do," replied Samira Awadah, Esquire, switching to Arabic as she said, "But just because I speak Arabic shouldn't be the only reason you hire me."

"No," Rania replied in Arabic, and then, after a pause, they both went back to English.

They set an appointment for Friday morning. Samira Awadah, Esquire, advised her that "both parents" should be present, but Rania only squeaked out, "I'll try. My husband just got back from an overseas trip. He has a busy job."

"I'm not here for you or your husband. My client is the child—I serve his interests." There was a brief pause. "My advice is that your husband should be there." Rania wished suddenly that she could be like this Arab woman—lean, strong. A woman who said to her husband, "You should be there," and didn't wait for an answer. Rania remembered how she'd worked, supervising an entire staff at the library, before it was clear that her son needed full-time care; she used to make statements, not suggestions, and now felt that she despised what she'd become.

This lawyer, she thought, will make sure what needs to happen will happen. And nobody will intimidate her. Not with those glasses.

When the call ended, Rania stood and stretched, then walked over to the couch. Eddie had fallen asleep, his face crammed down into one of the cushions. She shifted him to be more comfortable, then got a waterproof pad from the bedroom. Lifting his slim body carefully, she slipped the pad under his bottom. He was almost seven, and he hadn't had an accident in three months, and then six months before that, but she was still careful, especially with the new furniture.

She started dinner. Yousef was probably tired of Arab food after his week in Palestine—his aunts had probably served him mansaff and lamb and other heavy dishes every night—so she boiled some pasta and breaded some chicken to bake. Her phone rang as she was preheating the stove.

Her mother didn't even bother to say hello.

"Is it true, ya habibti?"

"Mama? Hi. Is what true?"

"Haven't you seen the posts? The hashtag?"

~~~

Later that night, she asked Yousef about it.

"There's something floating around on Twitter, habibi."

He glanced up from his laptop, his face tight.

"About your cousin Rasha. She died while you were there, right?"

"Yes, I went to her funeral. She died the day after I arrived."

"She died from a fall, you said."

"Yes."

"There's a hashtag—"

"What's a hashtag?"

He didn't do any social media. She'd joined Twitter and Facebook because of her job at the library, and later to communicate with autism advocacy groups.

She explained that everyone back in Ramallah and Jerusalem was talking about #Justice4Rasha. Everyone in Tel al-Hilou. She showed him some of the posts, mostly in Arabic but, in the last two hours, some in English too. He started sweating and pulled off his sweater. Her face was everywhere—the last photos of her taken the day before, while she was sitting with some friends. It was mostly social media stuff—there was just one small mention in an English-language Jerusalem newspaper.

But there were two articles written in Arabic on a website by an anonymous blogger, who called herself "Palestinian Athena."

She'd spent the afternoon, while Eddie napped, poring over the blogger's scathing corroboration of the allegation. "This must be investigated," she wrote, "or else the lives of women everywhere signify nothing." Rania handed Yousef her phone and watched his expression as he read; she knew the post by heart.

There had been no fall, Palestinian Athena claimed. Rasha's family had beaten her to death, crushed her skull in with some heavy object, then thrown her off a cliff. There was dust embedded in her scalp, above her left ear, Athena wrote, and that stone was found in the family's courtyard, not on the hillside. The fall had been staged later—the brother put her in a car, drove her to the edge, and tossed her dead body over. Her friends claimed Rasha was nervous about safety and never went walking alone. And why was she walking on that remote back road anyway? Why not take a stroll in the center of town, like everyone did? Like Rasha herself used to?

"We do not believe the family's story," proclaimed Athena. "We accuse them of murder. We demand #Justice4Rasha."

"This is bullshit," Yousef said; her phone shook as his hand trembled.

"She links to a video."

"A what?" he cried out.

Rania clicked on the video, the one the neighbor in the upstairs villa had recorded through her window. When it started, she left the room.

~~~~~

She'd heard it twice. The shaky picture was focused on the window screen of Rasha's family's house. Rania had recognized its ornately designed metal arabesques, the two tiers of steps to the front door. She'd been in that house a few times, after the wedding, when they'd visited Yousef's relatives. They had greeted her warmly and served her coffee, shai, watermelon, fresh grapes, cakes. She couldn't sit through another round of hearing the audio, the muffled screams coming from those windows. "God knows I am innocent" and "Please, Baba! Mama." Then a cracked, anguished, "Maaaa-ma!" The neighbor's voice herself whispering to someone beside her, "What the hell are they doing?" A man's response: "I should go see." The woman: "No, better call the police. The father is crazy."

No, she didn't need to hear it again. Instead, she sat in her bedroom, without her phone, idly dusting her dresser top with a baby wipe from one of the packs that were scattered in every room in the house. She drew the scented cloth over her perfume bottles, her wedding photo in a gilded frame, her jewelry box—she hadn't worn any jewelry since Eddie had been born. Only her wedding ring, a white gold band with a diamond that now seemed grotesque. She hated it because she'd sold herself for it. It wasn't the first. The first ring had been simple. This one had been a gift when she'd decided to stay home.

Yousef entered the bedroom and threw down her phone on the mattress.

She was afraid to ask him anything. She hated this feeling. She hated herself for feeling so nervous around him. When had she become this way?

"She fucking died from a fall. A fall!" He spat the words out. "As if it's not hard enough . . ."

"Okay." She refocused on the dresser, wiping it again and again.

"That blogger is a troublemaker! And that neighbor is a bitch. I have to call my uncle." He left her, rubbing anxiously at a spotless surface.

~~~

The first English-language article came out in a British daily online the same day that Rania met with Samira Awadah, Esquire. Mama texted it to her, adding: "What is Yousef saying about this?"

"He says it's a lie."

"Inshallah. I hope they're not responsible."

Rania sat in the elegant waiting room of the advocate's office, a room with olive-green wallpaper and mahogany furniture.

#Justice4Rasha. The hashtag kept spinning all over the internet, accompanied by a photo—it was a selfie, showing the young woman in the bookstore of her college campus. Smiling big, Rasha had looked rosy and sweet—a heart-shaped face, high rounded cheeks, and pretty, light brown eyes. Another graphic Rania saw over and over was an image of Rasha sketched in black and white by an artist, who had rendered her eyes wider, deeper, and more dramatic. Rania hoped she hadn't always looked that sad in her short life.

The advocate's secretary looked up from her computer and told her she would be called in shortly. "She's on the phone with a client," she explained politely. Rania, who'd started to stand, sat back down quickly and thanked her.

She tried to remember if she'd ever seen Rasha herself. Maybe they'd met briefly in Tel al-Hilou a few years ago, after Rania had married Yousef. She had traveled with him to Palestine that summer, before she was pregnant. The purpose of the trip was to meet his extended family who hadn't been able to travel to the States for the wedding. She remembered the family: Rasha's mother was a small woman with a stocky husband and several children. Four? Five? The article said Rasha had four brothers. She didn't remember them, or Rasha, but ten years ago, Rasha must have been a middle schooler. She probably played in the courtyard with the other children or helped her mother with a younger baby.

Rania remembered the uncle too, a tired-looking angry man who railed against Western influences. "And you, with your American jeans and your American phone," he'd said to Yousef, shaking his head in disgust. Everyone in the room had rolled their eyes behind his back. He'd shaken her hand too, and looked her over, as if she were another one of Yousef's Western colonialist accessories.

When she was finally called in, she stood again, taking the large accordion file that she cradled like a baby. So much of her life and work was carefully sorted and labeled here, under "Medical Reports," "Teacher Conferences," "FAPE," "School Accommodations," and more.

Samira Awadah, Esquire, was tall and formidable, with strong hands that gripped her own. "Let's see what you have here." She asked questions while sorting through her papers, occasionally asking for a document. Finally, she said, "You want him to move to first grade, yes?"

"The psychologist thinks he's ready."

"Do *you* think he's ready? Socially? Emotionally?"

She did. There was no empirical proof.

But there was this: yesterday on the playground, he'd awkwardly approached a group of girls on the monkey bars. They'd ignored him at first, but after a few minutes, he'd inserted himself into the circle until he was swinging along with them. Rania had watched carefully to make sure the girls were not laughing at him, but playing with him (they were). He just needed opportunities. She was sure of it. He needed to stay with kids his own age.

"Well, I'm ready to fight if you are."

"Do you think you can win?"

"Walou?" Samira burst out, in an insulted voice. Rania laughed aloud—it was astonishing to hear that word, which meant so many things. In one way, it reminded her of a sarcastic American expression she loved: "Do you know who I am?"

As Rania waited, Samira called the school and spoke to the principal. "I'm representing Edward Mahfouz, as well as his parents." And she set up a meeting for the following week.

"Will your husband be there?"

"I'll ask."

"You do that."

Eddie's birth may have been the last time she and Yousef were happy.

Strangely, his somber moods had seemed attractive. They'd met at a big Arab heritage festival in northern Virginia, the kind where the music blasted and the dabke lines spiraled across the dance floor like writhing snakes. She'd always been the type, despite living with a huge, rowdy family, to cling to the edges of a room, to watch from a space where a wall defended her back. That's where he was too. Before the end of the night, they had slipped away from the drumming and the dancing to drink a beer in the outdoor courtyard.

He had thick, curly hair that he kept pushing out of his eyes, and his front teeth were slightly crooked. One was chipped. After the wedding, he admitted he hated his teeth, but had never been able to afford dental work in Ramallah. "Do it here," she'd urged him, but he'd shrugged it off. America was all about work and saving for the future, not for indulging petty whims, he argued, seeming angry, as if she'd suggested something wrong or wasteful. All he had to do, he reasoned, was not smile too widely or too often.

Her parents had liked him, but Baba complained that he wasn't too talkative. "He sits in the room like a mouse," he said. "Tell him to be more sociable."

"He's an introverted guy."

"He's too serious."

"He's a good man, Baba. Leave him alone."

"He even dresses serious. Always dark colors."

"He owns a purple shirt now," she joked. "I bought it for him for Christmas."

But he changed once Eddie was born. His moods grew darker. She decided she could work part-time after the baby, and that became an excuse for his ever deeper gloom. "I'm just worried about money."

"But we're saving a ton on daycare. My whole salary would have been eaten up by it."

"I know. And you're doing a great job with him. You're an amazing mother," he'd repeated several times.

Until Eddie started missing milestones, and then suddenly she wasn't.

"He should know the letters by now. And he can't even hold a pencil properly to write anything. What are you doing all day with him?" The diagnosis changed little in his now-sunken opinion of her parenting abilities.

"This is not what I want my family to know about me—that my son is . . . deficient." He'd said this bitterly when they said Eddie had to repeat kindergarten. He'd said "deficient" like "cancer." An evil prank was being played on him. She'd reminded him over and over that Eddie was actually quite smart; the challenges made learning difficult, but not impossible. It didn't seem to matter, the irritability grew like a balloon until she danced around Yousef's moods, and then one day, while folding Eddie's laundry, while stacking his shirts in his drawer and bundling his colorful socks, she'd been stopped by a sickening thought: What if Eddie had been born with a severe disability? Something more challenging? Down's or cerebral palsy? What would her marriage be like then? She had no clear thoughts, only an image of herself, completely alone.

Yousef did not attend the school visit. Samira Awadah, Esquire, peered down at her and said, "This is very annoying."

She'd tried. She couldn't tell Samira Awadah, Esquire, the truth: that Yousef did not approve of her as their lawyer. "I know who she is . . . she divorced her husband, and now she's living with an American man. She's not married, but I think they have a child together."

"Oh." Rania had paused and collected herself with this new information. Samira was so private, guarded even, and maybe even more so because she knew Rania was Arab. "Even if that's true, it doesn't matter. She's an excellent lawyer."

"I don't like her."

"You don't know her," Rania had shot back, feeling angry. How dare he leave all the decisions in her lap and then question them. Yousef glared at her, but she calmly said, "I'm handling this, so just leave it to me." And that was all she could do.

Furthermore, this morning, he'd reminded her that Eddie was her responsibility. "You quit working even part-time, so that divided everything neatly. I manage what's outside the house, you manage what's inside."

Her parents had had a similar arrangement, she knew, but this still felt different. Mama, in her wooden slippers, had cooked dinner, shuttled five kids around to school and activities in her old station wagon, cleaned, went to parent-teacher conferences alone, while Baba rose before dawn every day to drive his food truck to the nearby college campus, where he sold egg sandwiches before 10 a.m., hot dogs and steaks before 2 p.m., and coffee and pretzels till 4. He then returned home, broken, so Mama could reassemble him slowly, carefully, with a cup of tea, by rubbing his temples, by putting her arms around his shoulders while he drifted off in a chair before dinner. After dinner, though, he'd be ready to play tawla and watch *Jeopardy*. By 9 p.m. he was asleep in his bedroom with the dark curtains. Those were the weekdays. But Saturdays and Sundays, he was all theirs—he would dust and vacuum and mow the grass, then help Mama with her grocery shopping. They shopped at the same wholesaler where he bought meats and bread for his truck. On Sunday afternoon, even when the temperature was frigid, Mama sipped her coffee while Baba grilled steaks on the deck, and the neighbors watched and shook their heads at their windows. That was a division, but there was also a blurring, a softness in the crossing over.

During the meeting, Rania listened in despair as the teacher explained how Eddie was socially "faltering." The principal then dropped the bomb: "We agree it's extreme to hold him back yet another year. That's why we actually believe we cannot adequately serve his needs here at our school."

Rania gasped. "You're kicking him out?" but Samira held up her hand, allowing the principal to explain how the school's limited resources prevented them from providing Eddie with the services he needed to be successful. She pulled out a list of other schools, where the county would bus him, that would be able to "serve his needs better."

Feeling sick, Rania turned to look at her advocate.

Samira Awadah, Esquire, was smirking.

When the principal had finished, Samira made no move to pick up the paper on the table. Instead, she calmly explained, "You know . . . and *I* know . . . that Eddie's requirements are hardly out of the ordinary. Moreover, he is legally entitled to them."

"Well, the fact is that . . ."

"I'm not finished."

If ice had a sound, it would be the voice of Samira Awadah, Esquire, shutting someone down.

Everyone's head jerked up just a little bit.

Samira Awadah, Esquire, continued: "It isn't, you see, a matter of *you*, as the principal, wanting but being unable to help. I assume that's where you were headed. Let me remind you, just so we're clear: Your job requires that you provide him with what *he* needs to quote 'be a successful learner.' And I'm going to make sure you do your job."

And that was it. They caved.

There would be future meetings, of course, but really, it was over. Because if it wasn't, Samira Awadah, Esquire, promised the county would find itself paying a hefty tuition bill to a private school that served students with learning challenges.

Rania got into her car and leaned back. Then she turned to the side and punched the headrest of the passenger seat, feeling the explosion of power in her arm. She drove, wearing a wide smile, to pick Eddie up from his class and take him home. She had not felt hope quite like this in a long time. He would move to first grade and get what he needed. As she drove home, she listened to him, strapped in his booster seat, explain the story they'd read today about caterpillars. "And *we* have caterpillars."

"Yes, we find them outside a lot, don't we?"

"On the steps. And on my swing."

"You like them?"

"I love them. I'm going to keep one."

"Okay, habibi. We'll make a nice home for it."

That night, more news surfaced: Another neighbor had made a video, the Palestinian Athena announced triumphantly, and she was making it available on her blog. The hashtag went viral again, carrying this new piece of the puzzle around the world.

Rania watched the new video attentively. The woman who lived across the courtyard had shot a sixty-four-second film of Rasha being dragged out of a car on the street and into the house by two of her brothers. She was screaming until one hand clamped over her mouth, and then the door shut. A blurred face appeared in the window, a man who reached up with both hands to pull the curtains together. Another scream could be heard until it was abruptly muffled.

"What are they doing—" asked a voice.

"God have mercy," mumbled yet another voice.

Baba called Rania by 6 p.m. to ask if she'd seen it. "Someone heard from the neighbors that they're going to exhume the body. What did Yousef say?"

"He's not home from work yet. I have to tell him the good news about Eddie first."

When Yousef came home, she told him about what had happened at the school, and he nodded, pleased. But his mood changed as soon as she showed him the video. Before it even finished, he was shouting at the phone: "What the hell?" Rania thought to herself that she'd never seen him look so out of control.

"Maybe they did do it, habibi. Think about it. Do you remember anything they said?"

"They *didn't* do it. I know them. I grew up with them. Would your brother ever do that?" he snapped.

"Of course not."

"And if someone is telling you he did, how would you react?" He looked at her in disgust, pulling on his curls. "Give me space right now."

She retreated to the laundry room. He'd barely seemed to care about their legal victory, coming alive only when he saw the video. She'd never seen him jump up so fast.

When she opened the washer, his own clothes from the trip were still in there, smelling of mildew. He must have washed them himself when he emptied his suitcase and forgotten to put them in the dryer. She reached in to pull some of them out, to see if she'd need to rewash them, and her hand pulled out a dark purple shirt and held it up. She stared at it.

"Oh . . . my god. My god."

She hurried out of the washroom, her heart beating rapidly. On the stairs, she broke into a run, barging in on Eddie, who was building Lego on his carpet. As Yousef stood in the doorway, staring in shock, she packed some clothes in a tote bag, holding her cell phone in her hand.

"I will call 911 if you try to stop me."

"What the fuck is wrong with you?"

"Stay where you are," she yelled, even as Eddie started to cry.

And then she grabbed Eddie and fled. As she drove, she called her parents and became hysterical.

"Pull over!" her mother demanded. "Pull over right now! The baby is with you!"

She turned the car into the parking lot of a pizzeria on Houston Street.

"The man in the video. The man in the window." She gasped as she spoke. "Look at the man in the window."

~~~

He called her throughout the night and into the next morning, but she allowed Baba to answer his calls.

"Well, she says it was you," she heard Baba say. "And when I look closely, it does look like you." Pause. "Maybe. There can be an explanation for anything. But they are here now. And they will stay here, and you will respect my house and my wishes."

There were laws, he argued with Baba. Rania had crossed state lines with his child.

"They're exhuming the girl's body today," she heard Baba say. "Worry about the law back home if they find what everyone is claiming."

She didn't know if Yousef would try to barge in one night and take Eddie, or hurt her, or even hurt her parents. So her brother Murad arrived with a bag and announced he was staying until the matter was settled.

On the third day, she called the school and explained they were out of town due to an emergency.

On the fourth day, social media reported that, according to the autopsy, Rasha had been pregnant. And Athena charged, more vocally, what she'd been alluding to for two weeks: Rasha had been raped, by her uncle.

That was the day Yousef wanted to talk. She told him he was on speaker.

"They only said they wanted to talk to her. They wanted all the family there. It's why they called me home." He paused. "She'd been hiding at a friend's house for a week—and she wouldn't come home. Maybe she knew. I've . . . I've been away so long. I didn't know how angry they'd be. I didn't know they were going to kill her."

"Who did it?" Rania asked, feeling sick.

"Wael hit her first. With the brick. But they all . . ." His voice trembled, then cracked. "They all took turns."

"Like an execution?" her brother cut in. "So there wasn't a single real man in that room, is what you are saying."

"Did you hit her too?" Rania asked.

"No! I swear it."

"But you didn't try to stop it."

"I did—but they were so angry, especially when she—" He paused. "She blamed my uncle. That's when Wael lost it."

"Maybe she was speaking the truth."

"My uncle didn't do it. I can't even blame Wael for that—imagine hearing your father accused of something so disgusting." His voice grew harsh. "She had a boyfriend, and she got herself ruined. She was trying to avoid the blame."

They hung up with him shortly after that, after Baba said calmly, "I don't trust my daughter's or my grandson's safety with you. They will stay here."

Over the next few days, as the police in the West Bank arrested Rasha's brothers, as the news story finally made it off blogs and into the *New York Times*, Rania understood several things.

That her marriage was over. Because she'd married a man who believed people could be ruined.

That he'd been called home by his family to handle or preside over a murder—that his mother had never been sick at all.

That he claimed not to have touched her in that room, after reaching up to close the curtains.

That she did not believe him.

"We need to stay here a while longer," she told her family.

"And to find you a lawyer, I think?" her brother said gently.

"I already know a lawyer," Rania said, feeling suddenly struck by the irony of it all.

"A divorce lawyer?"

"No. But she will know where to help me find one. A good one."

She went up to the guest room, where Eddie was watching TV. He showed her a jar he'd taken from his grandmother's pantry. "They have caterpillars here too," he told her. "Let's go find one."

"Good idea. And we'll drill holes in the lid and keep him in the jar."

"Yeah. But only for a little while. Then we'll let him go."

Behind You Is the Sea

Maysoon Baladi

When Reema tells me the lady lives in Guilford, I charge her an extra fifty dollars. My sister tells me haram, she's Palestinian like us, her parents are down-to-earth people, and God doesn't like cheating, but I answer that she lives in fucking *Guilford*. God understands.

I tell Reema I'll need the Buick two days a week starting today; usually, she needs it to get to her jobs, but she says she'll figure it out. Her day job is in the hospital cafeteria, and sometimes she can walk, but it's twenty-five degrees in Baltimore today. If I were her, honestly, I'd walk anyway. I can walk forever and ever. On most days I would, if it weren't for

Mrs. Alessandro's sons, who moved home last summer and spend all day drinking at the corner, whistling at all the girls who walk by like they didn't grow up with us. Mama worries about the Black guys on Charles and Thirty-Third and about the Spanish guys waiting in front of the 7-Eleven to be picked up (she forgets about Torrey). If Reema's son Gabriel hears Mama talking crap like that, he storms out of the room, but I'm more gentle. I tell her they're doing what I'm doing: hunting for work. It's not that dollars don't grow on trees. Maybe they do. But we don't even have trees in our neighborhood.

I wonder how Baba described America all those years ago when he sweet-talked Mama into leaving her village and getting on a plane to Baltimore. "Life will be so good, Allah kareem," he'd probably said. Maybe he'd even fed her the whole sidewalks-are-made-of-gold line. I'm just guessing. I have zero memory of Baba because I was a surprise baby, born fourteen years after Reema, and he died (probably of the shock) a couple years later. What I know for damn sure is Mama wishes she'd never left Palestine. She thinks America is one big trick that God played on her.

Reema remembers Baba. At fourteen, she was already pissed at the world. By fifteen, when Baba got sick, nobody could hold her back, I guess. "Mama didn't know how to handle me," she always says. "And Baba worked seven days a week in Mr. Ammar's strip mall, and then a second job as a janitor at the hospital. When Aladdin's was busy, he'd go there and wash dishes. So when he died? Who was gonna keep me in line?" It's the same hospital where Reema works now. They gave her the job because everyone remembered Jibril, the sweet old man with a cute accent who smoked cigarillos. "We used to ask him to say things like 'dry mop' or 'Clorox,'" they told Reema, going on about how funny it was the way he rolled the *R*s and *L*s. Reema thinks they're fuckers but the job pays thirteen an hour so she smiles and nods. That's how you survive when you need white people to help you—you just keep all the shit inside and collect your paycheck and thank God you can see the dentist once a year.

Right before Baba died, Reema met Torrey, who was sweet-talking and cute then, even though he's heavy now. Torrey's charm and green eyes are how we got Gabriel. Getting knocked up is haram but abortion is more haram, according to Mama. Gabriel was born when I was only three. So that's our family—me; Mama, who is basically a zombie that the neighbors tsk about; Reema; and Gabriel, who is seventeen and already has a mustache. And sometimes Torrey, when he and Reema are back on.

Torrey is in the kitchen now, scanning his Twitter and eating a bowl of cereal. "Where you going so early?"

"I have a job today."

"Not that crazy bitch on Falls Road?"

"Hell no." My last job was in a home where the lady wouldn't pay me, for the third day in a row, so I refused to leave. She kept screaming at me that her husband was *an attorney* and she was good for it, but she didn't keep cash in the house. When she actually called her husband at work to come deal with me, I got scared and called the only man I knew would have my back. And when her husband saw Torrey, he handed me three hundred dollars in cash and told me to get the fuck out of his house.

"Today's a new lady, in Guilford," I say. "Dalia Ammar. I think she went to high school with Reema. She's Palestinian like us."

"Don't mean shit. Sometimes you own is worse." He wipes a drop of milk off his chin with his sleeve.

"Her parents are nice people. Old school. But I guess she married up." Married way up, I think. Right up into the Ammar family, which owns a bunch of strip malls here in the city.

Torrey gives me a "huh" and shows me a funny gif on Twitter. It's a guy with his face in a mailbox: "When you just waiting for the refund check." We both snicker, and then Torrey stands up. "Okay, you need me, you call me."

"You working today?" I ask.

"Yeah, but I'm around. Happy to fuck with someone today." Torrey acts like a badass, because he is. When he walks by, Mrs. Alessandro's sons retreat inside her house. They don't want to catch a look from him. But I've also seen him cry when Gabriel got baptized, and I saw him weeping once in the hospital waiting room when Reema had an emergency appendectomy. That man leaned over his knees and sobbed like a child, and nobody in the world could console him until the doctor came out and promised Reema had come through.

I drive the Buick carefully. The upholstery is so old that the beige fabric is worn, pushing out stuffing like cellulite.

The exhaust pipe hangs like a pregnant belly, so I have to be careful on speed bumps. Reema bought it from the Bulgarian guy at work who washes dishes. He let her drive it for a week before taking our combined five hundred dollars.

At the light on Charles Street, I feel hungry. Last week, the Dollar Tree had microwaveable ramen, two multipacks for a dollar, and I cleared the shelf. But they're all gone now, between my addiction and Gabe studying for the AP exam late at night. I'm almost there, and since I'm early, I decide to get something to eat for lunch later. You never know if these people will feed you, even though you're giving them ten hours of your day. There's a small grocery store on Charles, so I pull into the parking lot between an Audi and a Tesla. Holy shit, I think, as I step out, making sure my car door doesn't touch the sleek red of the Tesla. Its door handles are flush with the side, and I wonder how you even get in. When I peek through the window, I see an iPad thing on the dashboard. It's so crazy that I keep staring. Suddenly, the handle emerges from the door, like some science fiction spaceship shit.

"Excuse me," says the snotty voice of a guy who's dressed like me: jeans, a T-shirt, sneakers. Except not like me, because he's so *branded*: there are logos all over his clothes, logos I don't even recognize, though I understand that I am supposed to recognize them—a lion, a tree, an alligator. This guy doesn't look like he's ever been one with nature. He's glaring at me while holding a metal coffee thermos that also has a logo on it.

"Sorry." I shut my own door by pushing down the lock and holding out the handle as I close it. An old white man smiles and greets me when I walk in. I pause in case he needs to search my bag, but as far as I can tell, this is his job: to say hello.

In the bakery aisle, I stand behind a woman in a skirt and heels who's ordering a loaf of something I don't understand. She turns as she waits, starts to smile at me, then looks me up and down and turns back around without completing the smile, so fuck her. Sometimes Reema doesn't know when people are looking down on her. I always do. I can smell the fakeness on people like celebrity perfume sold at CVS. I can sniff out the fragility that turns them nasty.

Behind a glass cage, there are cakes and Danish lacquered in glaze and egg wash, looking like little pieces of art. There's a loaf of focaccia, which I know how to pronounce because I subscribe to some foodies on YouTube; I make a note in my phone to find a recipe and try it at home. Everyone gets excited when I bake, because they know I can make anything. In the case there's something called an opera cake, which looks like a tuxedo, and a doughnut crusted with sprinkles that look like jewels. Also a chocolate tart with a juicy strawberry, like a raw heart, in its center.

"How much is the doughnut?"

Looking annoyed, the guy says, "Four seventy-five."

"For one?"

He smirks and points to a pretty blackboard in a white frame, propped up on the counter. The prices are chalked in different pastel colors. I walk away to the snack aisle, where I pause over granola that costs $8.98. A bag of corn chips is $5.98—the same brand they have at the CVS on my block, where they cost three bucks.

When I walk out of the store empty-handed, the old man gives me a gummy smile. As I drive down the street towards Guilford, I know there won't be a drive-through. This is not a value-menu kind of neighborhood. I'll prepare better tomorrow, after I survive today.

The streets in Guilford slide and curve like secrets, hiding homes from the public eye the way these people hide their money. I turn into Dalia Ammar's driveway and steer the Buick up the smooth blacktop, no cracks, no dips, thinking about how Mama goes outside at 4:30 every day and puts a chair in the street to save a spot for Reema. Here it's easy sailing, right to the top. The house is gray and white stone with shiny dark green shutters like dollar bills hanging off the facade. The glass sparkles on the windows, like eyes watching me. Around the front walk, I'm surprised to see clusters of daisies—something simple and sweet.

It's a double door, with a wreath bigger than my whole torso hanging on it. Before I can knock, a thin woman with sleek brown hair opens it.

"Assalamu alaikum—"

"Park in the back, habibti," she interrupts me with a

nervous laugh, and I'm startled. Arabs have a reputation for being hospitable, but I know, based on the church people, that this is a myth. I wonder if she doesn't want a shitty Buick to be seen in front of her house. As long as she pays me what I quoted, I'll park wherever the fuck she wants.

I get back in my car and follow the driveway behind the house. The lady has opened a back door, which leads right into the kitchen. "That's where you'll park every time," she says, standing at a wide marble counter the color of an elephant tusk. "I am Dalia. Imm Amir."

The kitchen looks like the ones in my YouTube videos, where the chefs have a huge counter like a canvas to make their art. The rest of the house looks like Dalia walked into a showroom at Pottery Barn and said, "I'll take it all." As she begins to give me a tour, I know I will do that thing I hate, where I'll go home this afternoon to our little apartment, with our mismatched Goodwill décor, and I will despise it.

She shows me the six bathrooms I'll be cleaning. She has three kids, two girls and a son, and each one has their own. She points out the crown molding that will need dusting in the dining room, the hardwood floors throughout, the silky white rugs. Downstairs in the basement, which she calls the "lower level," she shows me the theater. "This room is always a mess because Amir has his high school friends here a lot." The theater has eight reclining leather chairs with built-in cupholders and charger stations. She shows me the extra kitchen in the back wing. The outdoor patio with its brick oven.

"This is the workout room. It'll just need basic dusting," she says, pushing open a door and startling a man doing leg lifts on a machine. He's wearing shorts and a tank top. His head is shaved bald and his eyes are dark. And he looks pissed.

"Jesus Christ—"

"I didn't even know you were home," she snaps back. "This is the new cleaning woman, Maya."

"Actually, it's—"

"This is Demetri. Abu Amir."

"Sharafna," he says, standing and wrapping a towel around his neck.

"Come on. I'll show you the girls' playroom," Dalia says to me and marches away. Demetri turns without a word and adds another weight bar onto the leg machine.

"She's nervous," he says, not looking at me. "You're Arab, so she's worried you'll talk about her."

"I'm not like that. I don't even talk to most other Arabs around here, Mr. Ammar."

"Demetri," he says. He looks back and, because he smiles, I tell him my name is actually Maysoon.

Out in the hallway, Dalia mutters, "He's hardly ever here. Usually he's at work or at the narghile bar downtown."

"Oh? Aladdin's? My sister works a night shift there."

"Why would she do that?" Dalia looks horrified, and I'm not sure why I do this, but I say that I don't really go there. I feel it would make it worse if I told her my father used to wash dishes there long ago, whenever our food stamps ran out. That's what Mama and Reema told me—I don't remember.

Dalia nods as if she's accepting an apology. Her own parents are nice people, but her married family, the Ammars—they're not like mine; we're the family on the fringes that all the wealthier Arabs like to talk about. We are the "look what happened to" example. I imagine people telling their daughters, "Don't get mixed up with bad kids; look what happened to Jibril's daughter. She has a child and she's still unmarried. Her mother's touched in the head and her poor sister cleans houses."

~~~

Later, at home, I tell Reema about Dalia and her incredible house. "Twelve thousand square feet. Six bathrooms."

"These bitches, man." Reema sneers while making tea. She's between shifts: the hospital shift is from 6 a.m. until 3 p.m.; then she heads to Aladdin's from 5 until 10 p.m. "They marry rich to get out of working."

"Fuck that," Gabriel adds. He's at the table, studying for his AP Calculus test. His curly hair is gelled nicely, and he's wearing his Ravens jersey.

"Watch your mouth, ya haywan," Reema snaps.

"Watch yours," he returns with a smartass grin that makes me laugh and makes his mom yank playfully at his hair. "Yo," he says, pulling back his head, but she grabs it with the other hand instead and messes it up while he wails and I crack up harder.

"Now, ya shaytan. Now tell me to watch my mouth." Reema sets a cup of tea before him as he smooths his hair into place. "Get back to work." The AP Calc teacher is allowing only twenty kids in the whole school to even take the exam because she doesn't want to be embarrassed by the results. Gabriel's school is tough—most of the kids are on reduced or free lunch—but I know whatever it is, Gabe can do it. He started reading when he was three years old, just reading the headlines off the TV news like he'd been doing it for decades. Straight As for his whole life. When I'm baking, and he's around, he converts ounces and grams for me like a calculator.

"Why is this thing such a big deal again?"

"I can get college credit," he says. "That would save a few hundred bucks."

"That's cool," I say, remembering back to when I'd considered college. It's funny how you can grow up and never understand that you're poor. College tuition charts are the first clue. I gave that idea up real fast, even though Reema told me Baba had left some money for me. It's fifteen hundred dollars, and I guess I've always been saving it for an emergency. I bet Dalia Ammar has shoes in her closet worth more than that.

I thought I was smart in school, until I was doing algebra in sophomore year when Gabriel was doing it in eighth grade. I wrote essays quickly, turning in first drafts and earning Bs. The only math I liked was measuring in teaspoons and cups; my science was mixing flour and oil and eggs.

I pull meat out of the freezer to thaw for tomorrow's dinner, and Gabriel starts telling me about the schools he's looking at, while jotting down some combo of numbers and letters on his scratch paper. "I'm taking four AP classes, so if I pass all of them, I'd get a whole semester for free." He flips the paper over to use the back.

"You can do your first two years at the community college," Reema adds. "A lady at work can show us how you'd transfer later to the university."

"My counselor can help me with that," he scoffs. "I don't need Linda who stocks the salad bar." He's laughing but Reema looks hurt. "Sorry, Mama. That came out bad."

"That came out like *shit*," she blasts him, "because I stock the salad bar too. When it gets busy, yeah. I do."

He stands up. He's almost six inches taller than Reema, and he wraps his arms around her shoulders and kisses her head. She reaches up and messes his hair again, but he doesn't complain, just rests his chin on her head. After a few seconds, she pats his cheek and he goes back to his books.

"You should look at the community college," Reema tells me, her voice calm.

"Wallik, stop," I mutter.

We're quiet for a second. "Six bathrooms, huh?" she says.

"Twelve thousand square feet."

"Shit. I always knew she'd end up living in Guilford. She chased Demetri for years."

"I think they have problems."

"Oh, they hate each other. Dalia don't care. Everybody gets what they want, I guess."

I want to say that some people want only small, humble joys, but they get nothing at all. Instead I explain I'm glad her house is so big, because it means she needs me twice a week: one day for bathrooms and floors, one for laundry and dusting. "That's two hundred bucks. Cash."

"She's screwing you," Reema says, but I don't care.

"They need to raise minimum wage to fifteen an hour," chimes in Gabriel. "Bernie Sanders shamed Amazon into it. That's my debate topic for AP Government."

"Fifteen an hour? Maybe the new warehouse they built on Broening is hiring."

"That'll leave you with a broken back," says Gabriel solemnly. "I'm doing the research on working conditions now. You will come to hate your life, Maysoon."

I sigh and lightly smack the back of his head. "I already hate it. And I'm your aunt, ya haywan. Call me Khalto Maysoon."

~~~

Dalia's daughters, Hiba and Mina, take after their mother: they are complete assholes.

They have a trunk filled with Disney princess dresses: glittery, frothy things that are one-size-fits-all brats. They leave them, plus shoes, lip glosses, and their Nintendo Switches, everywhere when I am trying to vacuum. We all chipped in and bought Gabriel a Switch four years ago, and it stays docked and displayed on the TV stand like it's a statue of the Blessed Mother. I even dust the damn thing. In this house, I find the girls' Switches on the floor, the controllers detached. Dalia just says, "Laysh fi mishkalah, ya Maysoon? What's the problem?" when I tell her picking up their stuff takes me an extra half an hour.

The son, Amir, is a lot older than the girls. He's seventeen and Dalia tells me he's "going through teenage stuff," except fuck that because I've watched Gabriel grow up right behind me and he's never called his mother a bitch or slammed doors. Amir keeps his bedroom locked so I can't clean it, but Dalia says she'll unlock it when he's not home.

On Mondays and Thursdays, I arrive at the ass crack of dawn, because the first job is to put out the trash and recycling. Mr. Ammar—Demetri—is usually gone already, but once in a while, he comes into the garage holding his coffee while I'm pulling out the trash cans.

"Sabah al khayr," he says. "Thanks for helping us out."

"Sabah al nour," I answer. He actually looks at me when he's speaking. Once he asked me if Jibril Baladi was my father; I said yes, wondering if he knew about how Mama fell apart after he died. The church ladies like to talk about how she spent hours walking around the streets, pulling her hair, how Reema had to call the police a couple of times to help track her down. Social services got called once because I was a preschooler, and I'd get left home a lot by myself. But all Demetri says is that our dads used to be friends. "They hung out all the time at Aladdin's. You know, when it first opened, it was a coffee shop for the older guys. Now everyone goes there to smoke narghile."

Demetri says his father and mine once drove to Paterson together on a whim. "Just to buy knafeh."

"I hope it was good knafeh."

"There's no bad knafeh."

"I'll make some for you guys," I offer, and his eyes light up. "I make it really good."

On a couple of mornings, he seems to be just arriving home, looking like hell. He stumbles into their bedroom and locks it. Reema tells me he definitely has a girlfriend or two on the side. "Scumbag," she says.

Dalia doesn't leave the key for me like others do. Most leave it under the doormat. Some houses have a code, and they give me the digits. Not Dalia. She sits like the sun at her kitchen table, and I orbit around her, returning with gravitational force to ask her where the extra Swiffer pads are (in the cabinet), if I can use a scrubber on the oven top (no, it's sensitive), and whether it would be a good day to clean Amir's room (no, he doesn't want anyone in there). I realize she likes watching me work for her.

She looks up from her phone and her pastel leather binder to ask, "Yes?"

"I don't know where the shower cleaner is. I checked the closet."

"Maybe I'm out." She opens her binder to the shopping list tab and makes a careful note with her rose gold pen.

"So, what do I—?"

"Just use something else?" she suggests, like I'm an idiot.

This is when I hate her. What do I use? None of her stuff is Lysol or Clorox brand. It's all natural, infused with oils, in bright colors like bottles of fruit drinks. At home, I use baking soda and vinegar, the way Mama and Reema taught me, but if I suggest it, this bitch will give me the eyebrow. It's a tattooed eyebrow, and it scares me. Not physically, but like she will hurt me in a deeper way.

"I'll figure something out," I say and leave the kitchen. I end up scrubbing the shower with just water and soap. An hour later, I notice there aren't any tissues in the main bathroom, but I will be fucked if I go back to that kitchen. I look in the linen closet, then the girls' bedrooms, and then I open the master bedroom.

There, I gasp at the sight of Demetri on the edge of the bed, in his boxers. He looks like he's in pain, fixes his gaze on me while he strokes himself roughly. I freeze and he growls at me to shut the door.

I don't know why I slip inside, but I do. And I lock the door behind me. When I face him again, he looks delighted.

"Come here," he mutters.

"No." But I watch. The fact that Dalia is in the kitchen while I'm in here thrills me.

"Please." He grits his teeth.

"No."

"I need to . . ."

"Do it," I say calmly, though I feel dazed. "It's okay."

"Yes," he says, pumping his hand more aggressively. "Fuck, yes." And a few seconds later, his whole torso spasms, and he quickly covers himself with a wad of tissues. He leans back, his chest heaving. Before he can speak, I open the door quietly and hurry out.

In the hallway, I hear Dalia on the phone. "The meeting is at noon and we still need to book the caterer." When she hears me coming, she pauses her conversation and tells me in Arabic to make her an espresso. While I do it, I have to stop myself from giggling and trembling all at once.

~~~~

The next few times I arrive to work, Demetri is nowhere to be found. I haven't told anyone, not even Reema, what happened, maybe because I wasn't that shocked. I've walked in on Torrey doing it, though he yelled in embarrassment and apologized later. And I had a boyfriend years ago who liked to do it in front of me more than he actually enjoyed sex.

Reema has been busy anyway, because Gabriel is ramping up for the AP exam. The morning he's set to take it, we all flutter around like he's a soldier going into battle. Mama brews coffee and says prayers. Reema's up early before work, quizzing him while he eats the breakfast I made: manaeesh with zaatar. I make knafeh too, his favorite, and I prepare an extra tray to take to the Ammar family. "I got this," Gabriel tells us as he leaves, but he's nervous for sure.

When I get to work, Demetri is home, in the office off the

kitchen. He beckons me in. His desk is immense, the legs carved with etchings of leaves. He's on a phone call, on the speaker. A man with a deep voice talks about "zoning regulations" and some community petition.

"I need you to do these shelves, please," he says, pointing to them. He's going to act like nothing happened, so I follow his lead.

"These fuckers won't shut up," he says to me. I look startled, and he grins. "I'm on mute."

"Oh." I feel stupid. "Of course."

He leans in towards the phone and yells, "You bastards have no idea what I'm saying, do you?" And I'm cracking up, because they just keep droning on in their white-white voices.

"That's the only way I survive these calls," he says with a sigh.

I run my cloth along the wooden shelves. I take down the trophies, the plaques—Business of the Year, Better Business Bureau, Baltimore Community Philanthropy Award—and wipe them carefully. I've lingered over these before, when he wasn't home. There was a copper-plated plaque here last week that I don't see anymore. My eyes linger on the mother-of-pearl plaque in Arabic script above the desk. I run my fingers over the curved letters, swirling like little breaths.

"Can you read it?" I hear him ask behind me.

I read aloud and then translate it for him: "Behind you is the sea. Before you, the enemy." I glance at him then continue. "You have left now only the hope of your courage and your constancy." My formal Arabic reading is damned good, I must say. Baba taught Reema Arabic, and she and Mama both taught me. Not all the letters connect together—some have to stand alone—and that was the first and hardest lesson. But soon my skills became fire, and I was reading. The tashkeel vowels still mess me up sometimes, because they float above and below the other letters like they're flirting and playing all hard to get.

I'd seen this quote before, maybe in one of Baba's old books, but I hadn't understood the meaning behind the words until I'd googled them one night. That's when I read about the invasion of Spain and the famous speech by Tariq ibn Ziyad. He burned his men's ships at the harbor so they couldn't sail home; he'd known they were scared, so he made fighting their only option.

Why does Demetri have this plaque, I wonder? But I keep working. I'm glad it's not awkward between us, is all.

"I can't actually read it," he says thoughtfully. "I wish I could." I almost want to offer to teach him but I've already made them knafeh and that's enough giving for now. His wife can pay me more if they want me to be so generous with my time.

I continue dusting.

"Sometimes I'm on two of these calls at a time," he complains behind me.

"Wow," I murmur sympathetically, wanting to tell him Reema works two jobs in one day and comes home so broken and tired she can't eat. Arabs are ridiculous; even if they live a dream life, they want to star in some tragedy. If there is no tragedy, they imagine one.

"Where's Dalia?"

"Amir has a meeting with the academic coach." I reach up to dust the tops of the books.

"Maysoon." His voice grows suddenly husky, and so I turn. His eyes are intense, his pants are unzipped. The man on the call is talking about "marketing to the whole region" and "maximizing a convergence of strategies." "Stay where you are," he says, stroking himself. "Just let me look at you."

I drop the towel and lean back against the shelf. I'm not afraid of anything in this moment. I feel so powerful. On a whim, I reach up and pull the neck of my T-shirt down under my breasts, showing him my cleavage. His eyes bulge and his hand moves faster.

"Do it," I order him. "Now."

He grabs a tissue just in time, muttering "sorry." We say nothing. I finish the shelves.

Later, he finds me in the kitchen. "Maysoon, I feel terrible. Are you upset?"

"Do I look upset?" I'm shocked at what I just did, but I'm playing it cool.

"I'm not really sure," he says nervously.

There's no clear way to explain it, but for a moment, I feel we're the same. I tell him quietly, "If you need to do that sometimes, and I'm around, I don't mind. That's all I'm saying."

He looks at me for a few seconds, then kisses my forehead before walking back to his office.

When I get home that night, Mama is burning incense in the kitchen. The cast-iron bowl is on the counter, and she's burning yansoon and lemon peels. Her soft white church veil covers her hair, and she's muttering prayers in Arabic.

"He already took the test," I tell her. "He's sleeping in his bed."

"We have to pray before, during, and after," she says. "We surround him with prayers."

She seems so convinced of what to do that I'm jealous of her security, her faith. My eyes fill with tears and my throat feels itchy, and I want to ask her if she'll surround me too.

~~~

Reema's heard from someone that Demetri broke up with some girlfriend weeks ago. "He's such a dick," she says, flipping through the mail.

"His wife is a jerk," I say aloud.

"They're both trash." Then she groans. "Where is this fucking letter?"

"Dalia's son took it. He's waiting too."

"Right." She starts packing her lunch. "What's he like?"

"He's a little prick."

"Surprise. I meant Demetri. What's he like when you're in his house?"

"I don't know. I do my thing and leave."

"Good. Stay away from him."

Dalia eases up more about letting me clean while she's not around; she lets me in, then runs off to have lunch or attend yoga. One Wednesday, she tells me she's going to a ladies' society meeting. After she drives off in her Escalade, I head to the bedroom, where Demetri is waiting for me.

"Do you need to see them?" I ask. Last week, I showed him my breasts. And I kissed him.

"I need more," he says, stripping my pants off and patting his lap. "Come here."

Sex with him is slow and gentle. He keeps asking me if I'm okay, and he pauses to kiss me several times. His orgasm follows mine, and I feel him pulsing inside me. Afterwards, I start to get up, but he pulls me into his chest, like he's comforting me. "I think about you all the time."

I like when he says that, but I'm afraid to show it. I've gotten by my whole life by burying my hurt deep inside. "I need to finish before she gets back. She likes to complain how slow I am." Finally, he lets me go.

Later, I enter Amir's room, and the smell of weed hits me immediately. I open the windows, then pop my head into the office, where Demetri's on another call.

"It's muted," he says with a smile.

"Amir smokes weed in his room. Do you know that?"

"Shit."

"It's just weed." I shrug. "Could be worse."

"I don't even know what to say to him." He stretches his

arms over his head. "He and I . . . we're not close. He's a mama's boy."

I want to tell him a mama's boy doesn't take his mama's wallet and casually pull hundreds out of it, right in front of her face, or tell her to shut up when she asks what he needs it for. The things I hear and see in this house.

A week later, he reports that he talked to Amir. "He promised to stop. He's been stressed from school."

"Yeah. The AP scores should be in soon." When he looks surprised, I tell him Gabriel sat for the AP Calc test too.

He says he spotted Gabriel the other night, when he came to Aladdin's with Torrey to pick up Reema. "He's a good-looking boy."

"Well . . . you know." I use my hands to frame my own face and we both laugh.

"I wish you'd let me see you more. Outside the house. I'm not seeing anyone else." He's been calling me during the day, just to hear my voice. He calls me at night too, when he has trouble sleeping. He says, "I want to spoil you."

I tell him I've never been spoiled in my life and no way in hell will I get used to it now.

~~~

A few weeks later, the Buick breaks down on the way to Guilford. I pull over in the only place I can, the grocery store that sells million-dollar doughnuts. The engine keeps shuddering, so I shut it off. I call Torrey, who says he needs forty-five minutes to get to me. I text Dalia, "Car trouble. Will be late or can't come today. Sorry."

She messages back, "That's inconvenient." I think she means for herself.

She follows up: "Did you move my copper trays? The ones in the top cabinet?"

"No."

A heavy knock on my window startles me. It's the old man who stood smiling at the door last time. He's not smiling now. "You okay here?" He lets out a little hiss of air when he speaks.

"Car trouble. Someone's on the way."

"Well, you're taking up a parking spot here." Hiss. "Our lot is small." Hiss.

"Wish I could move it. But," I pause and wave my hand, "I cannot."

I roll up the window calmly and ignore his fat face, which looks like a hunk of white bread. He eventually walks away.

Demetri messages me. "What happened? Where are you?" I text back, and within ten minutes, his Audi parks next to my car. He grabs my cheeks and kisses me when I get in. "I got worried, habibti."

"Wow. That's sweet." I like how he says it. I look around his car, taken aback by the polished wood dashboard, the smooth gray leather interior. There's a sunroof that's pulled back so the light shines in on us both. "This is hot."

"I'm sorry about your car," he says, stroking my hand.

"This is going to be a shitty day." I sigh.

"Can Torrey just deal with the car? Do you have to stay?" He looks eagerly at me. "I could take you somewhere."

"And your wife?"

He shrugs. "She's going to tennis. Call Torrey."

Torrey tells me to leave the keys with the cashier inside the store, but I balk. "Can I just leave it under the car mat with the door unlocked?"

"Where you think you are, a little country town?" he scoffs.

When I hang up, I tell Demetri about the guy with the sliced-bread face. Looking pissed, he takes my key ring, peels off the Buick key, and steps out of the car. He returns soon, his face grim.

"What did you—"

"They'll give Torrey the key. And a complimentary sandwich. They're sorry for making you uncomfortable."

"What did you say?" I laugh as he backs out of the space and turns left onto Charles Street. "This is some *Pretty Woman* shit, right?"

"No. You're much hotter than Julia Roberts."

I insist on knowing what went down. "Maysoon," he says. "That building they're in? I own it, honey. I'm their landlord."

"Oh."

"I'll cancel my meetings. I'll take you to the Sheraton downtown for the day, yeah? We don't have to do anything. I'd love to even just take a nap with you next to me."

He wants to pick up something at the house first, he says.

In his office, he unlocks a drawer in his desk and pulls out a wad of fifties. He counts off a thousand dollars and hands them to me. I stand still while he kisses my lips, my jaw, the base of my throat. "Because you're so good to me. And I don't want you to ever worry."

I drop the money, which flutters to the floor. I'm not trying to be dramatic; I'm just shocked. Too shocked to even talk when he asks what's wrong. "I didn't mean anything bad," he says hurriedly. But I walk out of the house, down the driveway, and call Torrey, who meets me on Thirty-First and takes me to wait for a service truck.

I don't give up the job, because I'm not crazy, but the next few times I'm at the house, I ignore him as much as I can. I want to talk to Reema about it, but she'll call me an idiot. And I probably am one. It's hard to explain how he made me feel as cheap as my damned car. And just as broken.

~~~~~

Gabriel gets a 5 on the AP test. Mama is upset, but once we explain to her that this *is* the highest score he can get, she starts crying with us. Reema sobs against the counter. Torrey's crying too, but hoping we can't see while he thumps Gabriel on the back. We all feel it—it's a victory for all of us. The school counselor leaves him a voice mail, and when he calls her back, she says he might get scholarships to a four-year right off the bat.

But at the Ammar house, the next day, it's a different

story. Demetri's daughter Hiba is the one who tells me Amir "did bad on a test." That's my cue to avoid Dalia; plus she's slamming cabinets, emptying closets, just dumping stuff everywhere. I run the vacuum in the living room so I can't hear her sniping. I don't offer to help her because I'm going to be the one cleaning up the whole mess she's making.

"My silver narghile, Maysoon!" she calls out. "It has a big spout—the whole thing is real silver. I want to display it. Where is it?"

"I didn't see it."

"You know what?" She gets in my face. "Things have been missing for weeks now, and if you think I don't know what's going on, inti majnooneh!"

She's yelling and turning red, and they all come out slowly to listen: Demetri, the kids, like that opening scene in *The Lion King*, when the animals all gather. I'm the center of attention, and now she's stuck her finger close to my eyes. "Calm down, Dalia," Demetri warns. "Chill, Mama," Hiba says. Amir is quiet.

"All my stuff is missing! Do you think I'm a habla?"

"Yes."

She looks like a fish that Gabe had once; we kept it in a little glass bowl on the counter for a year before it died. Every time you'd feed it, it would swim up to the surface and its eyes would bulge out as it ate the pellets. Her eyes are like that now, big and round and lined with purple eyeliner like it's 1995.

"What's going on?" Demetri asks, coming between us.

He tells her to stop accusing me. Meanwhile, I give Amir a direct look, because I'm no fool. He glances away but I hold my gaze steady. He walks out of the kitchen.

"Dumb-ass kid!" I call after him.

"Who the hell do you think you are—" she starts, but I put a hand up in her face now.

"I'm leaving. Ask your son where he sold all your shit." I gather my things, and she follows me, telling me her son is smart and good and clean and and and.

"His shoes are better than your whole family!"

I turn around and walk right up to her. She backs up against the counter. "Shut your mouth. My nephew is his age and twice the man."

"Your *nephew*," she scoffs. It's so disgusting how she says those two words.

"My nephew who took the same test."

"What did he get?" she asks, her eyes narrowing.

I feel that same power, surging through me. She needs me at this moment. I smile coyly.

"What did he get?" she demands again.

I open my hand, my five fingers extended like a star. "The four-year schools are calling him about scholarships."

She looks like I slapped her. "Your sister the waitress who got knocked up in high school? Reema's son?"

"Reema's son who doesn't smoke weed and sell his mother's shit," I say, grabbing my bag. "That's the one." I slam the door behind me.

At home, Mama sits at the window, on top of a pillow on

the ledge, watching the street below. Reema is at work, and Torrey is watching YouTube videos on his phone and laughing. "Come and check this out," he says, holding it up for me and Mama and Gabriel to see.

I laugh, but I'm feeling quiet. I need to find another cleaning job fast, and I will. I always do. But I need to think further ahead too, because this day-to-day wears me out. I don't think my father worked his ass off in this country, and stashed away fifteen hundred dollars, penny by penny, so that maybe his daughter wouldn't be made to feel so cheap. It's like Torrey said just before I started working for Dalia and Demetri, "Sometimes you own is worse."

Gyroscopes

Layla Marwan

The cheering and clapping in the gymatorium make the wooden bleachers feel fragile, like the whole upper class might tumble in a heap to the basketball court. I'm in the middle of the row, so there is no way out for me without climbing over dozens of knees and ankles.

I stay put, quieting my heart.

It's the fall pep rally, and there are thirty minutes left. I would have hid in the library or in the physics lab with Dr. Bledsoe, but the school play will be announced here and no way I'm missing that.

So yeah, I can survive thirty minutes.

Probably.

My cousin Hiba cranes her neck, telling me Samantha is on the gym floor, leading a new cheer. That's when everyone starts stomping their feet on the bleachers, joining in. I check my phone to distract myself and see a message in the school portal from Bledsoe.

"Layla, considering a new project and need assistance," he says. "Come by this week."

"Will do," I tap back, just as a roar ripples across the whole gymatorium.

The basketball team has trotted out and they're doing some fancy dribbling. The varsity cheerleaders, in their tiny skirts, follow with a routine that is so haram it almost makes me blush. Even Principal McKenzie looks nervous. Samantha especially is writhing and trying to shake her ass in a pathetic way, her pom-poms on her thighs, an intense expression on her face, like she's stopped up.

"I guess she's trying to twerk," Hiba scoffs.

"She needs help," I reply, but inside, I marvel at her. I get uncomfortable when people look at me for any reason, good or bad. My Sitty Nadya always buys me pretty blouses and jeans for my birthday or Christmas, and Mama gets annoyed because all I wear are my big cardigans. I can't even imagine getting on a court in front of the whole high school and shaking my ass like that. It's crazy, but at the same time, I wish I had the guts to do it.

With ten minutes left, McKenz stands up and makes a few announcements, thanks all the coaches, then adjusts his glasses on his oily nose—I can seriously see the shine from here—and introduces Mr. Davison.

This is what we've been waiting for. Every year, when he announces the school play, he makes a big show of it. Last year, it was *The Wizard of Oz* and he hobbled in, dressed in a real tin suit, squeaking and banging his feet on the floor.

Two things to know about D: 1) he's our Drama Guild advisor, and 2) he looks like Andre the Giant, just with more expression. As our advisor, he's so much fun and knows so many weird facts. Last year, he made us watch *The Wizard of Oz* synced up to Pink Floyd's *Dark Side of the Moon*. He made it a mandatory meeting for all club members.

D glides theatrically to the podium, right under the basketball hoop. Lauren and I clap and root for him. He's wearing a long blue cape pulled tightly around his body. It even covers his face. He's so big he could probably just pick up McKenz and drop him right into the net.

I'm wondering what D is up to now when the sound system in the gymatorium booms with a loud clash of cymbals. A familiar song starts up—*Dat-dat-dat WAH WAH. Dat-dat-dat WAH WAH*—and everyone recognizes it all at once.

"Oh no," I mumble.

Cheers erupt around me.

Five minutes left.

D does a dramatic twirl and flips open the cape, and everyone screams. His face is painted blue. But of course, because it's D, there's more. He reaches under the cape and pulls out a white-and-gold turban and sticks it on his head.

"You know it! You know it!" he shouts jovially into the microphone. Samantha shakes her pom-poms wildly. McKenz and his shiny nose start swaying awkwardly from side to side. Later, I realize that the man was trying to dance.

My heart thuds out of control.

~~~

After school, Hiba and I go to McDonald's and each buy a dollar soda and a couple of dollar hamburgers. All we really want is the table. With an actual meal, we can sit for an hour at least before the manager tells us to leave. Hiba's mom is always putting her on a diet; at home, she has to sit with a salad and vinaigrette dressing while everyone else eats the regular meal, so she and I come here to fill her up before dinnertime.

As we unwrap our burgers, Hiba says, "They have a new movie now. It's not racist." She sounds annoyed.

I know what she means. In the live-action film, there's even a cute Arab guy playing Aladdin. Will Smith is the genie, so who can be mad at that? And Disney took out the lyrics about Arabs being "barbaric" and all.

I don't like this. Hiba and I don't really disagree about anything. So it's hard to explain how Jasmine makes me cringe. Jasmine's the only Arab girl I ever see in movies and she wears haram clothes and talks to a tiger. Hiba is chill, but her older sister, my cousin Mina, dressed up as Jasmine for years when she was our age. She was always going to high school parties dressed as a super-sexy Jasmine, with a tiny,

tiny top and lots of gold jewelry. Tons of white girls do it, but it's almost worse when the Arab ones do too.

And when white people hear I'm Arab, you can see their brains immediately jump to Jasmine, a princess whose father locks her up in a castle. Meanwhile, my baba likes to fix up old cars. We have a big garage at home and he puts his classic cars in there. He can spend a whole weekend working on them and, at some point, he realized I could figure things out too. Easy. "Layla, come here and try to take this out," he said one afternoon, in the summer. I was fourteen. He popped the hood on an old Corvette, and we both leaned over, studying the engine bay. He was pointing to the alternator. He didn't tell me how, just watched me.

When I finally did it, then he said, "Now put it back." So I did.

"Now this," he'd said another time, popping the hood on a Malibu. "Take out the AC compressor." Another time, he turned to the interior of a Mustang. He really trusted me by then. "See these seats?"

"Yeah?"

He'd handed me some pliers. "Take them out." And I did. My brain works like that. I can see how things fit, how they make sense.

I'm done eating, and I'm folding my hamburger wrapper into tiny squares, smaller and smaller until it's the size of my thumbnail.

"I just don't think we want to be the only Arab kids raining on the parade," Hiba says.

"I'm not trying to step on everyone here," I say. "I know everyone's excited."

I try to push down my annoyance with Hiba. I feel bad for her because she's always worried about standing out. That probably comes from her mom, Auntie Dalia, who is a diva like nobody you've ever seen. She makes my mom feel really insecure; it's almost like she's a parasite who feeds on other people's doubts. My dad always tells my mom, "Lamia, don't compare yourself to anyone, especially your brother's wife. That woman is ridiculous." But she triggers my mom anyway, the way she triggers her own daughter.

Hiba's problems also come from being the little sister of Mina, who was very popular, very skinny, very stylish. Hiba doesn't wear baggy clothes like me—I mean, she's stylish like her sister, but she is always worried about looking fat. Good luck taking a picture with Hiba. She will pose a hundred different ways, bending her knee, putting her hand on her hip, making you take it from higher up—all so she looks thinner. Sometimes I think she wishes she could disappear.

"Did you even *see* the new one?" Hiba asks me, guzzling the last of her Coke. As if that proves something. When I shake my head, she shrugs, like I'm an idiot. "So, you know, sometimes you can relax."

~~~

Dr. Bledsoe is like a caricature of a crazy scientist—his brown hair is never combed, and he's so skinny because he forgets to eat. I always think about how my mother would love to feed him.

When I stop by to see him after school, he explains that he wants me to help him build a gyroscope. I'm the only one in the whole physics class that he asked. "Is it for a grade?" I ask. I'm taking a full load of honors classes and nervous about taking on something that will hurt my grade. I need to keep my GPA up high for college applications next year.

"No grade, just for fun," he says. "Are you in?"

"Hell yeah."

Even when I was a freshman and didn't qualify yet for Bledsoe's classes, I would wander in and he would let me hang out in his lab. I'd clean the equipment and wipe the tables after school several days a week, when I wasn't in Drama Guild, and so I became kind of an assistant lab tech.

"Why acting?" he would ask me sometimes, studying a paper or peering at his computer screen through his tiny, rectangular wireless glasses. They looked funny sometimes, like two blank microscope slides, butterflying his nose.

"I like drama."

"Are you an actor?"

"Nah. I'm more behind the scenes." I could never risk acting: What if I forgot a line or made a wrong move? It would be witnessed by hundreds of people. Sometimes, I think that is why I like science. Science doesn't mind when you make a mistake. Instead, science gets kind of excited.

Before we start planning the gyroscope, Bledsoe shows me a video. "It's almost like an optical illusion," he says. I see a disk mounted on a frame, and it starts spinning wildly—but not really, I notice. There is stability provided by the frame, a force that always keeps it upright no matter how out-of-control it looks.

"It looks like it should be falling over, but it's not," I say.

"Like it's defying gravity, right?" He nods excitedly. "The torque applied to the disk causes a precession—so what happens is the axis is caught between gravity and its own angular momentum vector, and it's forced to find a happy middle ground to remain stable."

We watch the video quietly, like awed worshippers at an altar.

"I could buy one," he says thoughtfully. "I *have* money in the science budget. But . . ."

"Nah," I reply. "Let's build it."

~~~

D talks about the play at the first Drama Guild meeting after school the following week. He has pizza for us and cheeseballs and cans of Sprite. "We're asking four thousand from the PTA," he explains, "but they think we will actually make a lot of money on ticket sales." He's up on the stage, sitting cross-legged, on a long oak table, which is what we use to assemble and sew costumes during the year. Spreading his hands out, he says, "It's *Aladdin*. So yeah—everyone wants to see it."

There are two strategies, he says, to blow people's minds:

the genie has to appear and disappear somehow, using the fog machines, and the magic carpet has to be . . . magical.

"Can we build something?" He's looking right at me. "You know, to make it actually fly somehow? They do that in the Broadway version."

I'm sitting below him in the orchestra pit, with Hiba and Rajesh. Samantha is there too. Last year, she was Dorothy in *The Wizard of Oz*.

"Maybe. But actually, I was wondering . . ." I say, then add, "You know."

"I don't. Enlighten me," he jokes.

"Well . . . how *final* is the decision to do *Aladdin*?" My heart starts racing. In a second, my voice will tremble.

"Pretty final." His tone is curious, and he tilts his head as he looks down at me.

"It's just that, it's a movie that has a lot of stereotypes about Arab Americans, and—"

"Impossible. It was written in a time when there was no such thing as America," he says, laughing, and everyone else laughs too because now it's awkward.

He listens patiently, while I stumble through the little speech I practiced this morning. About the lyrics to the original opening song and how they painted Arabs in a bad way, and how it fed into the stereotypes that already exist about us.

Hiba is across from me, her eyes on the ceiling.

D is gazing down at me, his face attentive. But you know how you can tell when an adult is humoring you? Like, they're going to let you say your thing, and then they'll pretend to think about it?

He's pulling that exact shit on me.

When I'm done, he goes, "I appreciate you bringing this up." Looks all serious. He even hushes Samantha, who seems alarmed that the play is under threat. "In fact, I'm very sensitive to those issues and I've already considered them. And I made sure that the high school play script for *Aladdin* has no mention of those troubling lines at all."

"What were the lines?" Samantha asks.

"The song said Arabia is a land 'where they cut off your ear if they don't like your face,'" I say quietly.

"But they were changed?" Samantha asks D, and he nods. "Okay. So . . . that's good, right?"

D throws out his hands, like he's just done a magic trick. "Absolutely. And that's how it should always work."

"It's not just the lines . . ." I start to say.

But he's going on about being inclusive and how we have to listen to everyone's voice, except he's just ignored mine.

~~~~~

One day at lunch, I hear Rajesh announce he's auditioning for the part of Aladdin, and three guys, who are all in Drama Guild, roll their eyes. Because they know it's over. Rajesh is a great actor—he played the Scarecrow to Samantha's Dorothy, and he basically stole the whole show. He could have played the Wicked Witch and done it well. He just has a lot of charisma and a smile that could knock you off a chair because it's so hot.

"I might try out for the genie," Hiba says.

"Perfect," says Rajesh.

"That's okay, right? D didn't say it has to be a guy."

"The genie can be gender inclusive," he says with a smile. "This is a new era." He looks at me pointedly.

"I'm allowed to have an opinion," I say, starting to feel nervous.

"You are," Rajesh says. "But, like, if the show is offensive, I'd be offended. I'm Indian," he adds, like that explains it. And now the whole table starts talking like they're historians, about how the stories originated in China and India and they're not even Arab in origin. I hate when people bring up rebuttals that I don't know about, because how can I say if they're legit or if they're messing with me?

What I do know, sure as hell, is they are all making sure I know I'm wrong. How can I be right? My own cousin doesn't agree with me. The other brown person in the club doesn't agree with me. You're just the nerd who builds scenery, they're hinting.

I cave.

"I've been sketching ideas for a mechanism to make the carpet fly," I say quietly. They all pay attention. I am a team player, I say with my eyes as I explain my idea. I tell them how I researched the way it was done on Broadway. "It won't be anything like that . . . it probably can't carry anyone. But I think I can make it hover above the stage." I don't mention how, last week, I sawed some two-by-fours and hammered them together in a cross shape. I strung some heavy-duty wire to bind them and sat there, staring at it for a while.

I don't tell them how I thought, *This might work*.

I could make this work.

I'm just not sure I want it to.

~~~~

Mama tells me, "We never watched the movie because I hated it when I was your age." We're walking to the Enoch Pratt Library, which takes up almost a whole block on Cathedral Street. The front door looks like a massive fortress gate, and inside, the hallways are lined with statues and paintings. The best room is the Poe Room—Edgar Allan Poe died in this city, so they claimed him by naming the football team after one of his poems.

Mama brings me here a lot after school, because she likes to sit quietly in the big room and read a book. I need to study, so I come with her. We usually buy a hot latte at the café on the corner and sip on them while we work.

We find a table by the teen section, and we put our papers, coffees, and books down. "Mama, tell me . . . Why is it bad?" I ask her. "I'm trying to explain it but I get confused when they say stuff."

"It portrays Arabs as barbaric people."

"But Jasmine and Aladdin are characters everyone likes. They're not bad. And they're Arabs."

"They're also the 'least' Arab of all the characters . . . Jafar is very stereotypically Arab . . ." she continues, and then asks, "And why does Jasmine have to be sexy? Cinderella and Belle and Aurora—they're not sexy, they're pretty. There's a reason for that."

"Yeah, but . . . what's the reason?"

"Habibti," she says with a sigh, and I suddenly feel sad. If *she* can't even find the right words, what the hell can I do?

"Look," she says, "sometimes people just have to take your word for it. It's like someone stepping on your toes and not moving off. Do you really have to explain how the pressure is causing you pain?"

"Right."

"*You* don't have to prove it." She glances at me over her glasses. "Or agonize over how to explain it."

I talk to D during our Drama Guild. Someone has told him about my plans for the lift, so he wants to see my sketch. "This is how we can make it hover, maybe at a point when Aladdin summons it," I explain. While he reviews my sketch, I ask him, "Did you know there was a school that canceled *Aladdin* last year?"

"In Catonsville? Yeah, I know about that. It wasn't *Aladdin* . . . it was *Aladdin Jr.*"

"Same thing, though, right?"

"Basically. But they didn't even consult the parents.

Very disrespectful to the drama parents who, as you know, do so much for the club." He puts out his hands, looking like some wise Buddha. "The thing is," he adds solemnly, "everybody has a right to investigate other cultures and add their own artistic flair. Can you imagine if someone told me, because I'm white, that I'm not allowed to listen to or enjoy rap music?"

"Nobody is saying you can't read the *Arabian Nights*. But the—"

D smiled, like he was being patient with me. "You know, this cultural appropriation stuff wears me out."

~~~

Samantha and two other girls are trying out for Jasmine. Nobody else but Rajesh dares to audition for Aladdin, so he acts in the scene with each of them.

I'm still working on the pulley mechanism. It's always been hard to be the person D depends on for stage equipment and engineering. I watch Rajesh with Samantha, who's wearing a black wig over her blond hair, and she's dressed in a teal blouse and loose pants. She's really working for this one, I think. When she turns around, I see the black eyeliner dramatically sweeping across her eyelids.

She doesn't do too bad. She's always had the lead roles in the plays, since sophomore year. I only ever had one role, as a Munchkin, but that's because Allison got sick and I am the same size. They gave Allison's actual lines to someone else, and I was only onstage for a total of twelve minutes.

Rajesh steps offstage for a bit and smiles at me. God, he's so hot.

"You should try out for Jasmine," he says. "Your voice is terrific."

"Thanks. But I don't think so."

"So," he says, pausing for a beat, "this sounds weird, but you look authentic. If that makes sense."

"It doesn't make sense, because she's a cartoon," I say and go back to work on figuring out the pulley.

~~~

The gyroscope works.

Bledsoe is freaking like carbon dioxide gas bubbling out of a beaker. "I knew it," he says, slamming his fist down on the table. Except he does it weird, like he gets a strong windup going, but right before impact, he slows down so that his fist just gently taps the surface. It's hilarious.

"Amazing," I say, watching it closely. Honestly, the gyroscope looks like a bike wheel inside of a globe, but it spins magically, automatically righting itself whenever it leans too far forward or back. It just knows when to correct itself and pops back into alignment every time. I stop it and start it again with a flick of my wrist, over and over, taking a video for Baba. It never stumbles. It recenters and finds the middle, no matter how close it gets to falling.

It looks like a goddess being born, growing taller and taking shape, right there on the workbench, the round orb like a halo around her brilliant head.

"You know," he tells me, his eyes still fixed on the gyroscope. "I think you have a natural talent for science."

"I have a father who's an amateur mechanic," I say, "and I'm used to figuring things out." I glance at the time on my phone and stand up. "I need to get to D's room."

"They're still putting that play on?"

"Yeah." I pause. "I'm trying to tell them that I have a problem with it, but . . . They want me to explain *why*, and they want a reason, and D doesn't really want to talk about it. The whole thing just sucks."

He shrugs. "It does suck." He reaches out and sets the gyroscope into motion again. "The monkey was the most interesting character."

When I get to the classroom, there is a huddle of people in front of D's door, where a paper is taped. Samantha is there, being hugged by her friends, and there are tears in her eyes.

But she doesn't look sad at all.

Not at all.

I get closer and see, "Genie/Hiba. Aladdin/Rajesh. Princess Jasmine/Samantha."

Hiba is there too, and she slides her arm around me. "I guess she's the star again."

I knew she would be.

So why do I want to break something, as I watch Samantha fake-cry with her friends? Drama is not like science, where there's a right and a wrong. The test shows positive or negative. The experiment works or it fails. Either the thing spins or it doesn't. This is different and murky and I'm not feeling very good.

I go to my workroom and lock the door.

My heart is thudding in my chest, but I ignore it this time. It's not going to stop me.

The genie lift is on the bench. I can hear Dr. Bledsoe's voice, saying, "It does suck," and I continue to play his words in my mind as I use the brick hammer to smash the whole thing into tiny, jagged shards.

Cleaning Lentils

Hiba Ammar

On Wednesdays, Sits's house smelled like lamb stew, and on Saturdays like chicken marinating in sumac and lemon, the meat so tender it fell apart under the mere prodding of the fork. But that was it for meat—just two days a week. On all the other days there were lentils, brown, green, or red, simmering eternally in her grandmother's blue enameled pot, and the piercing scent of onions mingled with basil plants that grew in a row of pots on her flaking windowsill.

It made Hiba sick to her stomach. All of it.

The whole world conspired to make her fat. That's what it had to be. All that damned food sticking to her ass, piling up on all the layers of fat. And when she thought of her big ass, her gigantic ass atop legs that had no calves, her ass below a flat-chested torso, it made her even more disgusted. God and the ancestors liked to prank her—they'd sent all the curves to the wrong place.

Sits had given her a bedroom on the third floor. Even up here, the floor was tiled, so her bare feet, which also looked thinner, froze when they touched it. She'd called Sitti Maha "Sits" since she was a baby—it was the joke in the family, but Hiba had never stopped using it. There wasn't a single square inch of carpeting in the little townhouse, but tatreez draperies and pillows everywhere. Sits swept the whole house once a day; three times a week, she dumped a cup of lemon juice and a half-cup of olive oil into a bucket of soapy water, and mopped three floors of the house, plus the basement.

Sits looked like she'd stepped out of a different century. Every day, she'd drape a white scarf over her hair, which hung down her back in a thick gray rope. She even covered her hair when she cleaned, except then it was a bright green bandana that said "Mick's Bike Shop." She explained to Hiba, who had been horrified, that some nice boy in a black leather jacket had been handing them out on the street one day. She'd asked for one, and he smiled and gave it to her.

"He was laughing at you."

"No. I don't think so. He talked to me about this." She pointed to the rough cross and the lamb inked on the inside of her wrist. "He wanted to know who did it," she said and shrugged. "I told him in the old country, and maybe Jesus had one like it."

"I think he thought you were silly."

Sits shrugged, but she had a strange look on her face, like Hiba was a stranger.

She didn't know. She couldn't know. Hiba, coming off her own humiliation, lingered on Sits's ignorance of hers.

Seedo took care of the outside. Wasn't much of an outside, though. Her parents' lawn was huge, bisected by the most winding, curling driveway in Guilford. The front lawn of Sits and Seedo's house was Thatcher Street, which had four potholes that the city promised to fix and never did.

Thatcher Street and potholes and rowhouses and homeless people were why Mama had refused to live anywhere but Guilford when they'd gotten married. That's where Hiba had grown up, and it was very expensive. When Seedo once talked to Mama about how much she spends, she snapped, "Demetri is a rich man." And she added, "Why do you think I put up with him?" She didn't know they heard that, Hiba and her sister, Mina, but they totally had. So Hiba had grown up in the posh neighborhood, where the grocery stores had cafés and restaurants inside, and where your neighbors gardened for exercise but brought men on machines to trim the grass. In Guilford, the girls were all skinny. They all dieted starting in middle school, talking about Atkins and Paleo on the bus. Two girls, Mary Thomson and Jennie Stonefeld, were always fainting and loving the attention, but it was because they needed to eat. Alexis Moore was more yellow than white because she was so damn hungry. Here in her grandparents' neighborhood, the girls were more varied; Hiba watched them walking to and from school—tramping down the sidewalk in their boots, lugging their backpacks. Some of them thin, some athletic and muscular, some round and chubby. But here the fat girls wore tight leggings like the skinny ones and they didn't seem to give a shit how they looked.

Everything was strange here, but Hiba liked it. Here in Baltimore, the grocery store was a corner deli, where they sold one kind of milk, one brand of toilet paper. The only fruits came in cans in heavy syrup. Sits walked eight blocks to the open-air market for the fresh stuff, and once a month, she and Seedo took the bus to the other side of the city. There, between a synagogue and a strip of car dealerships, there was an Arab grocery store, where they stocked up on sumac, warak, cumin, and lentils. Hiba never went with them. She hadn't ventured past the front door since she'd arrived, but when they came home, loaded with bags and bags and Sits's metal shopping cart, she did help carry the lighter bags inside and stock the tall pantry in the kitchen.

"Why doesn't she go out?" asked the lady who lived across the street, the one with the flat-ironed blue-black hair and the penciled eyebrows. Her name was Liz, and she talked to Sits all the time, conversing across the narrow street. Hiba could hear them from her bedroom. She was so tired, but still giggled when they shouted to be heard over a car rather than pause their conversation, their voices rising as the vehicle chugged closer. "Did you get the COUPON FROM THE RITE-AID that came in the circular?"

"She visiting us." That was Sits's voice, so gentle but firm. "She student in za college."

"But it's November."

"She on a leetle break now."

The backyard of their house was something. Hiba had grown up with a magazine-worthy backyard, and she'd never once sat in it. There had been a small playset with a slide but Mama had had it torn down years ago, when Hiba finished fifth grade. "No need to keep junking up the yard," she'd said.

Seedo and Sits's yard was just a rectangle of cement with a table and a lounge chair.

But she came out here every day. And sat. Sometimes she cried, she thought about Snapchat and the texts and the whole last month and how she'd been brought to this. She was in Baltimore, for God's sake, living with her grandparents, who didn't even have Wi-Fi.

~~~~

A brick wall lined the yard's perimeter, and a small trough, built from cement blocks and filled with dirt, jutted out along one side. In one corner there was an apple tree, slender and fragile, growing out of a stack of black rubber tires, their centers packed with dirt like filled doughnuts.

Hiba sat in the lounger chair every day since she'd arrived, when the sun had gone down. She pulled her long sleeves over her wrists, her palms hunched down, cocooned in a sweater that had become oversized but that only last year had fit snugly over her breasts. Today, Sits found her there and set two cups of coffee on the table.

"Your parents called again." She spoke to Hiba in Arabic only.

Hiba answered in English. "I don't care."

"Ou wella bi him nee," Sits assured her patiently. *I don't care either.*

Hiba didn't bite. Sits had been trying all month to make her speak Arabic, ever since she'd shown up on her steps with her Coach suitcase and Tori Burch sandals on her feet. She'd also been trying to feed her obsessively. Mama must have told Sits about her weakness for rice, so Sits served it with every meal, either plain, or when that didn't work, colored with saffron, glittered with sauteed pine nuts, even sprinkled with cinnamon. But Hiba wouldn't touch it. She barely ate any of Sits's food at all, just pushed it around, made small hills of it on her plate, sitting quietly because Seedo insisted that if she wanted to stay there, she had to join them for breakfast, lunch, and dinner. She didn't have to pray, but she had to fold her hands and lower her eyes respectfully while they did.

"Any other rules? Anything else I need to do to stay here?" she'd asked that first night, sitting angrily on the kitchen chair, her forehead beaded with sweat. She'd brought a Get Out of Jail Free card, stashed it in her room. But she would let them talk, and say whatever they wanted, to think they were in charge.

"You can help with the chores, if you feel up to it," Seedo had said in Arabic. He was a tall, stout man, with a beefy chest and a thick white mustache. "Your grandmother is seventy-six now. I'm eighty-two. The garden needs work. The dusting needs to be done."

"Why don't you just hire someone, like my mom does?" She'd stared scornfully at Sits's hands, the backs of which were stretched and shiny like wax, the veins bulging on her forearms. Hiba's nails were usually polished and neat, because that's what Mama expected. She'd had her first mani-pedi when she was ten, and every two weeks since. Here, though . . . here was different. Hiba's nails were chewed and bitten, eaten away the way she wanted to devour herself, devour her pain. It made her laugh to think how Mama would grimace if she saw them.

"Hire someone? To clean my own house?" Sits had looked incredulously at Seedo and chuckled. "Istaghfurallah." Seedo smiled too, his white mustache curving like a tuft of snow settling on a tree limb.

"Fine. I'll do chores. Anything else?"

"Yes." He stared at her somberly. "In this house, we smile. So you have to smile at least once a day." He burst into rumbling laughter at her surprised look. "Seeing you in our house is like waking up to a dream. Stay as long as you like, angel."

She thought about his words now, as she sipped Sits's coffee. How they'd struck her as weirdly sentimental. So awkward and earnest. Her grandparents spoke in casual poetry, dropping phrases like "you're blooming today" and "you bury me because I love you so much." They always, always, always called her habibti and ya ayooni. My love. My eyes. The fact was that she wasn't used to this, this awkwardly normal way of discussing intense emotions. Mama and Baba were more formal. More reserved. Baba only used flattery with waitresses and hotel clerks. But with her, they were like teachers, where caring for you also meant always assessing you, grading and judging. "Watch your expression," Mama always said. "Keep your head high. Remember who you are." It was why, over the years, they'd rarely seen Sits and Seedo, who frowned openly at the way their daughter was raising their grandchildren, at how she had seemed to forget where she came from.

~~~

Jennie texted her on the Saturday of her third week.

> You okay? Haven't heard from you.

>> Staying with relatives. Taking the rest of the semester off.

> Dina's taking over your space.
> Wanted to see if you're okay.

>> All good. Just need time off.

> Glad you're okay. Your rents okay with time off from school?

	? Don't care.
K.	
	Yep.
She's loving all the extra dorm space. Bitch.	
	I bet. Bitch.
She got the whole bathroom now.	
	She needs it with that ass.
LMAO. He's in there every night. Probably eating it.	
	Daniel?
Yeah. He's a slut. He'll fuck anything that moves. You saw the shit he posted that time?	
	Yeah.
That poor girl.	
	Yeah.

~~~

During week three, Sits told Hiba she needed her help with cleaning the windows. This meant moving all the knickknacks—the porcelain Victorian ladies, the picture frames, the vases of plastic flowers—off the windowsills and wiping them down, then standing on the sill and Windexing the glass top to bottom. At her parents' house, there were windows that were twelve feet tall, and that men came with ladders and sponges on poles to clean. But Hiba obeyed Sits, because when Baba had told her "enough is enough," and "get your pathetic ass out of my house," it was only Seedo who'd said "come."

There was one photo of herself, her sister Mina, and their brother Amir—all in their Christmas outfits—flanking her parents in front of the tree. Mama's "Macy's tree," Hiba always called it. She must have been about ten in the photo, and she looked like a goddamn whale. Her sparkly gold dress made her look bloated, especially next to Mina, who always wore sleek black dresses on the holidays. Hiba picked up the photo and carefully moved it to the side, then climbed up on the sill.

She stood carefully, aiming the spray bottle of blue cleaner up at the top. She started to rub the bubbles with her towel, when Sits stopped her. "No," she said in Arabic, "we don't want streaks." Then, carefully, she coached Hiba how to wipe down, down, in one smooth motion, then move back to the top of the window. When it was finished, she stood there, her body in the window frame, and looked down at Thatcher Street, at the girls playing double Dutch. One of them, with long blue-tipped braids, was in the cage now, her chubby stomach and thighs bouncing as she jumped. Her mother sat on her stoop, smiling and clapping along with the beat for her. When she messed up, her ankle catching the rope, her mom clapped even harder and shouted something that made the girl flick her braids and smile. Hiba wished she could go down to the street and rewind it, to hear the words that the mother had said.

"Khalasti?" Sits asked her. "We have two more rooms."

"One more second."

"What's wrong?"

Hiba continued looking at the girls. "Can you throw away that picture of me?"

Sits picked it up. "No, I love it."

"I wish you would." She climbed down carefully, her arms not as steady as they'd been in the past.

Later that night, when all the windows sparkled and Sits and Seedo had gone to bed, she carefully removed the photograph from the glass and completely and cleanly cut her body out of the picture.

~~~~

One day, Seedo requested her help. "I'm tired," Hiba said, lying down on the couch. She slept here a lot, in the midday, wrapped in the numerous blankets that Sits crocheted. Her favorite was one of multicolored, mismatched yarn. "This one is so warm," she told her grandmother. "But the pattern is strange."

Sits had shrugged. "I had a big box of leftover yarn. So I kept crocheting until I had none left." Hiba loved that she could understand Arabic better since moving in with them. Now Sits looked suspiciously at Hiba. "You know, I made you a blanket when you were little. For your tenth birthday."

"I don't have a blanket from you."

"A big light blue and gray one?" Sits stretched out her arms. "It's for a twin bed—so big."

But Hiba had never seen it.

"Humpf," Sits had snorted, then gone back to stirring the lentils in the pot.

But Seedo made her shed the blanket, put on an extra sweater, and come outside. He wanted her to work in the garden.

"You don't have a garden," she explained to him calmly. He raised a palm to his heart and looked offended. "Ilsanik," he chided. Your tongue. But he was laughing, and she laughed too. It felt so strange, how much they laughed. They didn't have cable or Netflix, or goddamn Wi-Fi, but they told each other jokes and laughed all the time. One day, Seedo had said he felt like eating lamb, and Sits had reminded him it wasn't Sunday. "But I feel like having it," he said stubbornly, winking at Hiba, and Sits's response had been a cool "I'll make it at your funeral."

"What am I supposed to do?" Hiba asked him now as he handed her a trowel.

"Dig holes here, about six inches apart," he instructed her. "And we're going to plant these." He pointed to a flat cardboard box, like the kind they hauled apples in from the outdoor market. It was filled with clumps of dirt.

"You're going to plant dirt?"

He looked up at the sky. "They claim she's in college, heavenly father," he spoke to the clouds.

She tried not to, but in spite of herself, Hiba giggled.

His head snapped forward, and he winked. "This is garlic." He fluttered his hand around the dirt in the box, shedding it to reveal white bulbs like curved, ivory fangs.

So they squatted before the trough of dirt, and she used the trowel to dig holes. Her arms ached and, at one point, they shook from the exertion. Seedo said softly, "It's okay. It's good for you. This is like exercise. Make you strong."

"Make me have an appetite?"

He grinned and winked. "Your mama—she's smart too."

Hiba turned her attention to the dirt. Everyone said that about Mama, but she wasn't smart, Hiba thought. She was just busy. She acted busy. She looked busy. Sitting on the boards of charity groups. Going to fundraiser galas anywhere between DC and Philadelphia. She always said Baba had made his money in real estate, not in something like medicine or law, so she had to make up for that lack of prestige in this way. Every time she said it, Baba stood and left the room.

Hiba had always hated Mama's charity work. Once she got a community service award at some fancy party in a ballroom, Hiba and Mina had to dress up and be shown off like an accomplishment. Their brother had been there too; this was before Baba had sent him to rehab for drugs. Mama hardly ever talked about Amir, and when she did, the story was that Amir had somehow betrayed her.

Hiba scraped her finger on something sharp, a shard of wood. The skin separated and the blood ballooned out in a big, fat drop. "I'll be back."

"No, just wash it here, with the hose."

"No, Seedo." She shook her head. "I need a Band-Aid."

There was a shelf in the bathroom where Sits kept extra towels, cotton balls, Band-Aids. But she heard a noise in her bedroom and walked in. Sits had her hands in Hiba's top drawer, digging under the bras and T-shirts. Hiba could see her mattress had been moved, the sheets messed.

Sits slowly withdrew her arms. She held the bottle of pills in her closed fist.

"What the hell."

"We were worried. We told you not to bring anything that could hurt you."

"I'm leaving."

"No," Seedo said, from the doorway. "No, angel. You're staying here until you're better."

~~~

What's up with Dina and Daniel, she texted Jennie.

> He posted a pic of them trashed. From last week.

Smart. Right before finals.

> Yeah, they're both idiots. I told her to be careful. If he posted the pic of that girl, he'll do something to her too.

She listen?

> Doubt it. She's a bigger skank
> than he is.

One morning, Hiba's cheekbones pushed out against her skin. They'd been disappearing these past three weeks, as she'd been lulled into Sits and Seedo's quiet life. But now they were back, jutting out sharply, like marble, giving her face a distinct, sophisticated, sharp look. A look that said, "Stay away from me, or I will hurt you too."

She thought—not for the first time—that she looked scary.

Had she appeared like this to Daniel? She'd struggled so hard, and it hadn't been good enough anyway, but now she wondered if she had been pretty at all. Maybe he didn't care—the picture hadn't been of her face, after all.

When he'd leaned over her after, while she slept, what had he thought? When he'd raised the camera, what had he hoped to capture? Something gross? His caption had said, "At the beach, bitches." Because there she'd lain, like a big whale on a messy bed, her back to the camera.

Sits always liked to touch her face, to tug affectionately at her hair, to say "jameela"—beautiful—several times a day. That's how she was. Always touching. Seedo too—he kissed Sits's hand every time she brought him a cup of tea, patted her shoulder whenever he walked past her. Without thinking, it seemed. It's just how they were.

How had Mama grown up in this house? Hiba imagined her as a little girl, being carried on Seedo's shoulders, being wrapped in a handmade blanket on a cold night, having two people worry when she got sick. She imagined Seedo getting up early to sponge brown dye on Mama's school shoes then smooth it through the leather so it gleamed. Had she hated this life? Is that why she threw out any shoes with a scuff? Any sweater that sprouted a thread? This was not poverty—not the kind she saw in her textbooks, or the kind that they talked about at the galas on whose boards Mama served. No swollen stomachs here, no famine, nobody swatting flies and walking to the well for water. What had made her the kind of mother who assessed each one of them before they left the house, making sure their hair was stylish, their makeup right, their handbags and shoes Prada or nothing? A woman who'd once tossed away Hiba's craft bin when she'd started painting T-shirts with puffy paint for fun. Who'd insisted on hair relaxers to ease the frizz. Who had a manicurist on call at the salon in case she chipped a nail.

Sits noticed her cheekbones. She ran her waxy palm over them. "Ya rouhi, ya rouhi," she said. A few minutes later, Hiba watched her burn incense in a black cast-iron bowl and mutter prayers over it. She took the smoking bowl upstairs, and an hour later, when Hiba went to lie down in bed, she smelled its aroma everywhere—her sheets, her closet, her dresser—a sad, sweet smell, like something she missed.

She wanted to say to Sits:

You're so good to me.

I think you're beautiful. Your gray hair like steel, the wrinkles at the corners of your eyes, the shuffle in your walk—it's the purest beauty I've ever seen.

Sits, she wanted to say, I hate the way I look.

She focused instead on being here in this house. On the concrete moments. Touching the tiled floor with her bare feet. Listening to Liz shout at Sits across the street. Watching Seedo through the kitchen window as he hunched over the apple tree, tying it at one point to the fence to keep it upright when it was about to collapse.

~~~

"You need to go outside and walk a little bit," Sits said during week five. She'd received an application form from her teachers to request a semester extension, but she hadn't filled it in. She hadn't even read through it.

She'd only been going outside to sit on the lounge chair, soaking up the light like a human solar panel. Sits had taken away all her long-sleeve shirts, but neither she nor Seedo said a word about her thin arms. She'd also hidden all the knives in an overly dramatic move, but Hiba didn't blame her. She heard Sits talking on the kitchen phone to Mama, asking her what she should do. "No, no, she can stay here as long as she wants. But I'm worried. Wallah, I'm scared for her."

It was really bright and sunny the day that Sits insisted. They walked to the produce market, and Hiba pulled a metal cart behind her.

"Look at these," Sits said, running her rough hands over a bin of cucumbers. "They're cheap and they're small, like the fakous we eat." She looked at the burly man behind the stall. "Hello, Mauricio," she said in her English.

Hiba stood quietly, her hands deep in the pockets of her hoodie. The sun filled her eyes and she didn't have shades, so she pulled her hood up and over her head.

"Your granddaughter?" Mauricio asked.

"Hiba. Yes." She patted her chest. "Ma do-tur's girl."

He nodded at Hiba, but she smiled back in a quick way then ducked her head again. The glare was making her eyes water.

"My grandson . . . he help me too. Good boy, he works with me."

"That's good boy."

"How many you want?" He smiled at Hiba. "You need a lot. You gotta feed this one. She too thin."

Sits asked Hiba if she'd like to try them and she nodded just to say something. She really wanted to go home, to her little clean room on the third floor, where everything smelled like lemon and wind, and lie down in her soft bed where the scent of incense lingered a week later. She didn't want to imagine Daniel in her old dorm room, climbing into Dina's bed the way he'd climbed into hers, kissing Dina and telling her she was beautiful, as he'd told her. He wouldn't ever. She was sure of it.

"How about these tomatoes? These look good to you, habibti?" Sits held up a dark red one, like a softball. Hiba peered at it, squinting. "I'll get a few, yes?" Sits smiled and Hiba could tell she was worried. She'd gone back to not eating at all in the last two days, since Jennie's text. She'd picked at small fragments of her food, enough to keep the acid down, but her energy was draining. What had she eaten yesterday? she wondered, as she watched Mauricio bag some tomatoes. Half an apple. Ten almonds. A piece of chicken the size of her thumb.

Jennie hadn't figured it out. Snapchat got rid of it, but surely someone . . . someone had figured it out. Her hair had been spread across the pillow . . . not many girls on campus had hair like her.

Farther down the stalls, she pulled Sits's metal cart as her grandmother loaded up on green peas, bananas, and potatoes. Hiba had not eaten a potato in two years, not since senior year of high school, at Jennie's graduation party. She wondered what Jennie was doing now. Probably studying for midterm exams. Maybe planning the Thanksgiving bash on campus. Maybe sitting on the quad, eating her pho from the takeout place, not giving a shit that she'd gained twenty pounds since freshman year.

Hiba's head buzzed. As they turned a corner to visit a new row of stalls, the sun hit her harder than ever. This row didn't have the wide umbrellas that the others had, and the glare lasered down on her full force.

"They have fresh apricots, habibti," came Sits's voice, seeming far away. There was a lot of noise, but from where? Hiba squinted through the yellow flashes before her eyes, swimming in heat, and registered—right before she collapsed—that Sits had started to scream.

They told her that Mauricio and his grandson had lifted her like a feather into the backseat of Mauricio's car. The doctor in the emergency room said she was severely dehydrated and she found herself on an IV. They couldn't find a vein in her inner elbow so they punctured one in the back of her hand, and then began forcing her body to accept calories.

Sits and Seedo sat on the chairs in her room, pecking away at the cell phone they shared. It was a flip phone but they texted on it anyway, hitting the number keys repeatedly until they reached the letter they needed. When they left the room to huddle with the doctor, she took the phone they left on the side table. Using her free arm, she scanned their messages.

She sick. Come.

> She does this all the time.

Need you.

> It's her drama. If we come,
> she'll know she won.

Haram.

> She wants attention.

She desirv it.

Mama and Baba did not come.

Instead, they sent Mina.

Mina, a younger, less plastic version of Mama, swung into the hospital room carrying an expensive bag and wearing tight jeans and beaded sandals. Her eyebrows had been tattooed on her face that summer during a trip to Beirut with their cousins. Hiba hadn't been invited. She'd never been Mina's choice of a friend. Mina felt the same about her—she had no doubt. Mina, for sure, felt she'd been dealt a bad hand in getting a depressive dud for a sister.

"The doctor said you're underweight," Mina said, perching on the chair. "Tell them you'll start eating more and they'll let you go."

"Okay. I will."

"Make it believable."

"Yep." She was too tired for Mina today. Or any day.

Her sister noticed the faded vinyl purse on the floor. "Is this Sits's?"

"She went for a walk with Seedo. They come at eight every morning and stay all day."

Mina saw the cooler with the wheels and looked at Hiba.

"They bring their own food," she explained. "They don't like the cafeteria food."

"There's Uber Eats. Or Grubhub."

"They have a flip phone, Mina."

"Fucking Christ." Mina snickered. "How do you deal with them?"

"They're fine," Hiba said, suddenly annoyed.

"You're so weird, Hiba." She readjusted herself on the chair. "You could have just come home. Mama and Baba aren't mad. Just embarrassed."

"Right. Okay."

"Mostly Mama. Baba's worried about you and wants you to come home."

Mina's eyebrows looked like two sword blades, about to cross each other. She looked like a monster, with her carefully lined lips and her skin coated in primer and contouring makeup. A clown in some sick nightmare.

She leaned closer to Hiba. "So. You had a boyfriend. And he dumped you. Big fucking deal."

"It was a big deal." She looked at Mina's manicured pink nails, thought about Daniel's fingers pinching her waistline.

"Get over it."

Hiba wanted the bed to either swallow her or snap together in half and kill her.

"There's a silver lining, right? You lost some weight. That's good. Now just don't overdo it."

The fingers in her right hand, where the IV pierced her tissue-like skin, looked like the chubby worms she'd had to dissect once. That was in high school, where she'd first realized she was fat. The soft curves of one's upper arm were no longer sweet. Having a butt that filled out your jeans meant you were a pig. Eating in front of other girls was a disaster. Everyone was on a diet and nobody was ever hungry. She'd eaten half her sandwich, then a bag of chips one day, and by tenth period, her new name was "Hippa." She'd carried it through graduation.

But college was a new beginning. And she'd lost weight over that summer, getting in shape for her freshman year. That fall, she'd met Daniel, when she thought she was finally trim and fit. Except after she'd let him fuck her, her first time, on her bed in her dorm room, with Jennie in the next room, he'd run his palm over her belly and said, "You need to get this under control." She'd tried. Because she craved having someone like Daniel put his arm around her in the student lounge, in front of everyone, having him kiss her on the quad while people walked past. For once, people looked at her like she was more than just a brown girl with frizzy hair, more than just the girl you asked for the class notes. She was attached to someone. She belonged to Daniel. And she wasn't about to give it up.

And then one morning he left, and after class she'd seen her picture—the picture of her bare ass in bed—on his Snapchat. He never called or apologized. The dorm buzzed for a week about whose ass it was. Jennie asked if it was hers, and she said no. It turned out he was fucking two other girls, so hardly anyone knew about her anyway. And the most pathetic part, she thought, before having a breakdown in her room and swallowing the pills, was that she'd almost been glad because that was the slimmest her ass had ever looked. And she'd had pretty dimples above it, the way skinny girls did when their jeans hung low. When she woke up in the hospital, she refused to be released to her parents' home. Mama had looked almost relieved.

"Mama said if you want to come home, you should. She's

just telling everyone you're doing some kind of yoga retreat thing."

Hiba decided that if the bed didn't swallow her or do her the favor of killing her somehow, she'd make herself disappear. She'd done it before, when she'd heard girls gossiping about her ass in study hall, or even when Mama had tsked over her taking a second helping at dinner. "God, that shit wiggles like Jell-o when she walks." "Do you really need that, Hiba? It will take you an hour on the elliptical to burn it off."

She'd cocooned herself in silence during those moments. Now she did it again, by imagining herself in the small backyard, by the odd apple tree, in her worn hoodie, sipping Sits's coffee. She became the tree, slipping into the hollow center of the black tires, sinking into the soil. Mina's words couldn't scale this. Her sister talked, tried to wring a compromise out of her, but Hiba remained silent until Mina shook her head and finally left.

When Sits returned, she sniffed the air. "Who was here? Your mother?"

"Mina."

"I smell her perfume." She coughed. "Did she leave any in the bottle?"

Hiba stayed quiet, wriggling her fat fingers, making the skin on the back of her hand stretch painfully.

"It reeks of arrogance," Sits muttered in Arabic, then cried in alarm at the choking sound coming from the bed. "Habibti, what is it?"

Even Hiba needed a few seconds to recognize the sound of her own laughter.

~~~

"They want to come and see you. It's Eid al Milad." Sits was a Christmas maniac. She started decorating right after Thanksgiving with her embroidered tatreez tablecloths and runners.

"I don't want to see them."

They were sitting in the yard, and snow had dusted everything, even the leaves of the apple tree. It was still standing because Seedo had tethered it to the wall. But with its white coat, it glistened like an angel. It could be a Christmas tree, if she hung some decorations from it.

"You should," Sits said. She held two trays, filled with lentils, on her lap. She set them on the table, one in front of herself and one in front of Hiba, then began picking her way carefully through them. "Look for small stones or dirt."

Hiba obeyed, watching how Sits's fingers scurried across the pan, sifting and inspecting. Her knobby fingers were graceful and light.

"How do stones get in there anyway?" Hiba asked, reluctantly pulling her hands out of her sleeves and stretching her arms across the tray. She imitated Sits's small, precise movements—pushing the lentils all to the front of the tray, and pulling them back as she filtered them.

"They just do. And I have to make sure they're clean before I cook them."

"My mother never cooks addas."

Sits snorted and paused to sip her coffee, then went back to picking. "Food is love. You have to pass your love into the food," Sits said solemnly, like she was reading from her Bible. "We lived during three wars. Lentils kept us from starving. Your Seedo and I—we love eating them. It reminds us of those days."

"Why would you want to remember? If they were such bad days."

"They were terrible," Sits said, nodding. "But it's good to remember. So you can look at your life now and say alhamdulilah."

Hiba continued steadily picking, watching how Sits's fingers worked so swiftly, flicking through the dry beans, clicking and shifting them across the wide aluminum pan, separating out the stones that would hurt you from the lentils that could save you.

Worry Beads

Samira Awadah

In less than twelve hours, Samira would be forty. At work, Maysoon, her new assistant, had already started with the "Over the Hill" and "End of Youth" jokes, but those didn't rattle Samira, whose life had actually ended a decade earlier, before she'd turned thirty. It had come as a massive crack that cleaved her bone in two jagged halves—the before, the after, and if you were lucky, there was sometimes relief from the pain of separation. Bones could reset, yes, but even now, the space where the fibers had fused together throbbed like a painful memory.

She stood now in the backyard of her sister's Baltimore

home, watching several men erect a tent. The party was not for her, of course. She'd arrived early to help and been told Baba was wandering again. When the truck had arrived to set up, she knew he needed supervision. So she was out here, watching the tent's metal frame rise up on the grass like a large silver skeleton. She wondered how it didn't crack—the frame bent and dipped and almost folded, but no, she thought, amazed, it stayed firm in its nakedness. A few minutes later, the men in red uniform shirts preserved its dignity and honor by clothing it in white canvas sheets. Off to the side, Baba was also watching, looking both amazed and amused at once. She watched the men finish dressing the frame like a bride and found herself wondering, not for the first time, why the party was never for her.

Her brother-in-law Muneer rested a cooler of beers on the grass. "Big four-oh tomorrow, no? It had to happen sometime."

She didn't admit, especially not to him, that there had been a point when she'd suspected it wouldn't, rainy days when the healed bone of her arm ached like it had been newly broken. "The tent was a good idea. Especially since you're having a lot of people."

The tent dominated most of the small yard, although Muneer had claimed a space towards the back for the lamb pit. The neighbor's son had been hired to watch so the meat didn't burn. He sat by it lazily, drinking beer, though he looked only fifteen; with his other hand, he cranked the bar as the animal, skinned and impaled on a rod, rotated over the low flames like a sacrifice.

Baba, tired of the tent, now stood calmly by the lamb, watching it turn. His hands were clasped behind his back, holding his masbaha, fiddling with the beads. They were his oldest strand of beads, the rosary he treasured because his own father had made it by hand, carving the beads out of olive pits.

She approached him, and he asked her, as if they were already in mid-conversation, "Why are we here again?"

She reminded him that her twin nieces, Sarah and Dunya, had made their first communion.

Baba's eyes, beneath the tufted white eyebrows, were fixated on the flames with an intensity that worried her. Her mother, as usual, had driven him over and left him, returned home to get herself ready in peace, practicing eagerly to be a widow.

"Baba," she called to him. "Stay back from the fire."

"And just so you know, Samira," Muneer said kindly. "They won't be coming."

When she stayed quiet, he ridiculously added, "You know who I mean, yeah? They're on vacation this week." She continued to ignore him, and he shrugged and walked away to check on the music.

The twins were setting up soda bottles and plastic cups on one of the folding tables that lined the yard's perimeter. Muneer and Ruba had six children—the twins had been a double surprise. Samira had offered her sister that mabrouk with a broken, humiliated heart. Her jealousy had sat like a swollen, scalded tongue in her mouth.

You're celebrating with these girls today, she chided herself now. Smiling at them and glancing over to make sure Baba was safe, she bent down to fill her cup with ice from the cooler.

"Coming through, Miss."

A large, tall, bald man stood behind her, carrying a stack of folding chairs. Four chairs, bundled together, and he was holding them under one arm. Four more under the other arm.

"Miss? Do you mind? Sorry, these are heavy."

She scooted out of his way, quietly delighted by his "miss." She'd remember that tomorrow when she woke up in a new decade.

He set the chairs down and then grinned at her, his face sweaty. His skin was tanned, making his blue eyes even brighter.

"Thought I was gonna drop those for a sec."

"I'm sorry."

"I'm the one who's sorry. We're a little late delivering these. Your party starts soon, yeah?" He flipped the chairs open, one by one, and slid them under the round table, like petals on a flower. "Had a guy quit on me this morning. That's how it goes sometimes."

"That's terrible. Can I get you a soda? Water?"

"I'm fine, but thank you," he said, nodding at her appreciatively. "Very nice of you to offer."

As she poured Diet Coke into her cup, he told her, "We can come back in the morning for everything. And you don't have to worry about cleaning anything. We do that."

"Good of you."

"We aim to please. Best rates in the city." He said this teasingly, smiling flirtatiously at her.

"I know," she said. "I paid you."

He scrutinized her, narrowing his eyes. "So you're S. Awadah. The address on the check didn't match the delivery address."

"Samira."

"Logan."

She took a sip and answered the question that lingered. "It's my gift to my nieces. My sister organized everything, but I paid for the party."

"So you're the nice aunt, then? Bet you're the fun aunt too." He winked at her, and she flushed like a stupid teenager.

~~~~~

The guests arrived, including Mama, who sat like a queen on the padded lawn chair, smiling, chatting, giving not a single thought to her husband, whom Samira had to pull back from the flames twice. At least seventy people were crammed both inside the house and under the tent. The band was a local group of Arab college students who played the oud and banged away on the tabla. Samira helped Ruba refill the trays of rice and chicken and restack paper plates and napkins.

And then they came.

She couldn't believe it. Despite what Muneer had promised, they streamed in through the back gate, carrying a bottle of wine, kissing everyone hello. They'd just gotten back into town that morning, they claimed, determined not to miss the party, istaghfurallah.

Samira shrank back behind the deck's sliding glass door, feeling sick. She hadn't seen her ex's brother in years; he had a booming voice and a thick mustache like Jerome, and his wife and children followed him like a pack of starving puppies.

The way Jerome had always expected her to trail him.

Samira retreated to the small family room towards the back of the house. "Schway schway, ya bint," she told herself. In the wine cabinet was a bottle of simple red, one she'd bought Ruba and Muneer last Christmas. Still uncorked, which meant Ruba was saving it for important company. Feeling vengeful, Samira found a corkscrew and opened it. She grabbed one of Ruba's good wineglasses, filled it, and settled on the couch.

To wait until they left, or until she could sneak out unnoticed.

As she sat, she heard the tabla, the chatter, the laughter, the "ya habibi"s and "salamat"s. The sound of people who'd had a pleasant week, and for whom a backyard party under a tent made for a lovely end to it.

What seemed most unfair was that she couldn't even be angry at Ruba. Jerome's brother's wife, the puppy, was Muneer's second cousin. Marriage was a wide web, and divorce's threads were sticky, impossible to completely escape.

Baba ambled in just then, looking overwhelmed. She patted the couch, and he came gratefully, his masbaha clutched in his fingers.

"Are you tired?" she asked him softly in Arabic.

"La, ya binti," he said, patting her knee comfortingly. "I can stay with you. Don't worry."

"Who am I?"

"You're my Samira."

Maybe Jerome's brother wouldn't stay long, she thought, as the minutes passed. But every time she stood and peeked through the kitchen window, there he was.

"You're hiding," Baba said, as if it were very natural. "Your mother keeps hiding my papers. She doesn't want me to go home." He sighed. "You need to talk to her for me."

Her niece Sarah wandered in just then, wearing her white communion dress. "There you are. They're dancing, Auntie."

"Oh, good."

"Come dance with me."

"Not now." She was on her second glass.

"Please. I don't want to dance with anyone else." Though Samira had fourteen nieces and nephews, Sarah was her only godchild. She was the younger twin, a bonus baby, offered in pity to the barren sister.

"Go enjoy yourself," Baba said, patting Sarah's head.

"Who is she?" Samira asked him.

"Isn't she your daughter?"

She closed her eyes for a moment. His memory swung so drastically, between lucidity and complete invention. The first time he'd asked her why she was not yet married, she'd felt slapped. You couldn't depend on him anymore, on knowing for sure that he was with you. He was like a drowning child, sometimes thrashing above the surface, sometimes slipping, before you could grab his hand, into the depths. As she heard the music get louder outside, Samira thought angrily: she'd paid for this goddamn party, whether Ruba told anyone or not. They were all out there, eating her food and drinking her beer.

Sarah led her out to the yard. Logan's crew had set up a wooden dance floor too, and she began to sway her hips. Sensing the presence of a skilled dancer, the young drummer intensified the beat, like issuing a challenge.

She met it. The long, deep blue fabric of her skirt swayed with her, hovering in an arc long after her hips had fluttered to the other side.

One of the few times people noticed her, she knew, was when she danced. Even Jerome, usually stingy with his compliments, had told her once, "You move like a dream, and you're built like one too," while sliding his hands up her dress on the ride home from a party. That night, years ago, when she'd danced, a small circle had formed around her, and the drummer had run out, dropped to one knee before her, his palms buzzing over the tabla. It had turned Jerome on like a gas lamp—when they'd pulled into the driveway, he'd dragged her up to the bedroom. Not that she hadn't wanted to. But she'd wanted the gentleness, the easing into it, that Jerome in his impatience had never tolerated. Later that month, when her period had started right on schedule anyway, Jerome, who'd been sure this time had worked, had slapped her. And when she'd been too stunned to respond, to fight back, he'd let go, his hands drumming over her face, her back, her thighs, places that would turn blue overnight.

She swayed now, amazed by how these memories could still suffocate her. She finished the song without looking once at Jerome's brother or his family, especially not at his wife with her thick, angry eyebrows. People clapped and Sarah hugged her. Samira headed back to the living room, settled back next to Baba, and finished the rest of the red.

A shrill beeping shocked Samira awake. Her brain vibrated against her skull. She struggled to open her eyes, wondering where she was and how her lids could be so heavy. She rolled over, falling onto the ground. Not far. Not a bed, then. A couch. She peered around and saw Ruba's flat-screen TV, her coffee table, her dining room.

God, the noise.

She was still fully dressed, without shoes though. Where were they?

Samira tracked the noise, opened the kitchen door, and walked out onto the deck, pushing her long hair off her forehead. A large box van rolled backwards on the grass, then halted before the tent.

The beeping stopped.

"Good morning, sunshine."

Logan stood on the grass below her.

"It's too early to be so loud," she said, her voice raspy. "People are still sleeping—"

She saw two other men come out of the truck, nod to her, and stride over to the tent. She waved awkwardly.

"It's nine fifteen. Gotta take down the tent. Can't sleep the day away," Logan teased, his voice softer as he approached the patio. He stood right underneath her now. She could reach down and pull his hat right off his bald head.

So she did. The hat sailed through the air and landed on the grass.

"Someone's hungover," he announced, looking amused rather than annoyed.

"I am not."

"No big deal." He shrugged. "Wear it like a badge of honor."

She glared at him and walked barefoot back into the house.

Everyone was asleep. Ruba and Muneer's bedroom door was closed, and all the children were dozing in their beds. She didn't want to be here, especially not in Ruba's house, when she was feeling so disoriented. She'd never felt safe here. She needed to be home, the home she'd bought, far away from them all.

Her damn shoes though.

No matter. She had her purse. Fishing out her keys, she left the house, locking the front door from the inside, and trudged carefully, barefoot, out to her black Audi, a treat after making partner. Her mentor at work had gently advised her, "Samira, you know you can't pull into the executive lot now driving an old Camry. You gotta play the part." She'd been grateful: she was climbing mountains and didn't always know how the ropes worked.

The Audi was parked in front of Ruba's ugly mailbox; the red flag on it had been broken for years, decapitated by a drive-by. Fumbling with the key fob, she saw Logan approach, wearing his hat.

"Leaving the scene of the crime?"

He stared down at her feet then let his gaze move up her legs, her waist, linger on her breasts and her face.

"Heard the front door shut. I came out to apologize." He hesitated, then asked, "Don't take offense, but you okay to drive home?"

"I'm fine."

"I can take you."

"Really, I'm fine."

He nodded uncertainly. "Wait here a sec?" and he hurried around to the back of the house. When he returned, he was carrying a paper cup of coffee with a new white lid. "I just picked this up for myself. Haven't touched it." He held it out to her.

"Oh, no. I couldn't."

"I remember your address, from the check. Bethesda is forty-five minutes from here." He pushed the cup into her hand. "It'll really help that headache. Trust me."

She peeled back the flap on the plastic lid. The first sip felt like a magic potion, soothing her throbbing head. "Thank you so much."

"Drive safe. I gotta get to that tent."

He smiled at her again and headed back to the yard.

She climbed into her car, sipping the hot coffee. Later, as she merged onto the Beltway, she remembered that today was her birthday.

~~~

She'd bought her house because of the walled garden. Normally she spent Sundays out there, checking emails and enjoying the sun. Today, the light was too much for her so she stayed indoors, watching Netflix and dozing. Nobody in her family called. Sarah texted a simple "Happy birthday, Auntie." She read it, texted back a smiley face, and put her head down again.

She'd been advised, "Making partner means you don't get a day off. Not Saturday. Not Sunday. Christmas morning—maybe."

There were consequences. On Monday morning, when she arrived at the office by 6:30 as usual, she found 214 emails in her in-box. As she sat there, two more popped up, making it 216. Most were about the ADA compliance suit against the local school system, her first major case in this new position.

She opened the first email.

By 11 a.m., she'd gone through three-quarters of the messages. Before her regular Monday staff meeting started at

11:15, she brewed coffee in the break room and stretched her back.

You okay to drive home? I can take you.

The Keurig hissed. She took her coffee and disposed of the pod.

Flirting had been fun. Knowing that he was a gentleman who would have driven her home—that had felt so damn nice.

Her staff surprised her with a small birthday cake in the conference room. She knew Maysoon had planned it, and so she sat quietly as they sang weakly to her. She blew out the single candle and handed out slices. The meeting itself was tense, and she fielded some criticism disguised as feedback from Rebecca, who'd been trying to make partner for years. She kept her eyes leveled on the woman and refused politely to change her deadlines. Pushing deadlines back would make her appear to be struggling, and she knew that trick.

Years ago, after her arm had fully healed, she'd gone to Ocean City, Maryland, stayed alone in the beach condo of a sympathetic friend. She stood in the water, feeling the waves grow stronger. They pretended to relax her, but they really pulled her, with their subtle pressure, their gentle shifting. It was a lesson, and she learned to keep adjusting, making sure she never was forced to move from her original spot.

When the meeting ended, she noticed a text from Ruba.

Meet for lunch?

Busy day.

> A quick one? I'll come to the place in your lobby.
>
> Everything okay?
>
> Baba.

When Samira saw her sister seated at a table by the window, she wished she hadn't agreed to meet here. Ruba looked very much like a frumpy mother of six, in her yoga pants, with her messy bun. She wore lipstick—overly glossy, swiped on too quickly.

"Muneer was upset yesterday morning. You drank so much."

"I don't normally do that, Ruba."

"The kids, Samira—"

"Well, did I do anything stupid?"

"No," she admitted. "Baba saw you passed out. He got nervous. Mama had to yell at him to make him leave." She paused while the server took their drink orders, then resumed. "We have to talk about him. Mama can't keep doing this."

"She doesn't do anything."

"Be nice."

"His hair is long and his nails are longer."

"She's tired, Samira. You have to understand."

"Whatever." She read the menu. "I'm getting a salad."

"Are you losing weight?" Ruba asked peevishly.

"I don't think so."

"So I'll call you soon to plan a time to meet? With Mama? We need to figure something out."

They ordered, then proceeded to ignore the main topic. Instead, they talked about the party. The food had been plentiful, the twins had looked lovely, the crowd had stayed till almost 1 a.m.

"And you put on quite a show, like a belly dancer."

The food had arrived by then, and Ruba dove into her Reuben sandwich, dipping the side fries into ketchup.

"By the way, I *really* didn't know Bashar and his wife would be there. They answered no to the evite."

"I don't care."

"Anyway." She leaned in. "So Bashar told everyone that Jerome's wife is finally pregnant."

Samira picked up her knife and cut up the greens of her salad mercilessly.

"Good news, right? After seven years of marriage, mashallah."

"I guess so." Plus two years to me, she thought. And four more with the second wife. Lena was his third.

She finished her salad, wiping the corners of her mouth with her napkin. Ruba chattered on about her summer plans, talking even though her mouth was full of food. The twins wanted to do an art camp. "It's at the university. And expensive, so." She looked up at Samira. "Who knows?"

"How much?" Ruba told her. This was their routine. When it was over, Ruba would pretend to want to pay for lunch too, and when Samira refused, she'd invite her over for dinner one Sunday "after church." Even though Samira hadn't attended church in fourteen years. She'd never found

God to be very helpful. Going to the twins' communion had been a major compromise.

"Let me treat them. Eight hundred dollars isn't that much."

"For one week?" Ruba shook her head, as if scolding Samira for splurging. Samira almost admired the look of dismay Ruba had perfected years ago, marveling at how she'd been easily portrayed as the bad one in this negotiation.

"Send me the bill." She picked up the black folder with the check.

"Let me get that," Ruba said, reaching for her purse.

Samira toyed with her, silently watching while Ruba waded through packs of wipes, stray receipts, and a box of crayons. "You sure?"

"Oh. Yes, of course, you do so much for us," Ruba insisted in a panic, pulling a McDonald's toy out of her bag and staring at it in surprise.

"You know what? I insist." Samira put up her palm, getting to the close of business more quickly. She disliked her sister, but she hated the bitter aftertaste left by acting petty. She said goodbye in a hurry, so Ruba wouldn't have time to say something insincere like, "Are you sure you're not upset?" She'd spent her whole marriage pretending not to be upset. It was inappropriate to look upset. Or seem upset. Or act upset. Trashy, wallah. Those things did not suit a newly married woman, and they made other people uncomfortable. So the question was always insincere, because the expected answer was "I'm fine, alhamdulilah." Nobody wanted to hear the truth. Truths were complicated, stubborn things, especially when they festered openly, refusing to heal.

At three o'clock that afternoon, she finished reading the 216 emails, plus the 38 that had come in since the morning.

Leaning back in her chair, she studied her hands. They were tanned and unpolished. Bare of jewelry. And they wouldn't stop shaking.

~~~

When her phone rang that evening, she was on her couch, in her perfectly ordered home—the home where every pillow, every vase, every rug was exactly where she'd placed it or ordered it to be placed.

"Wanted to make sure you were feeling better today," Logan said. "I . . . I got your number off the invoice. Hope that's okay."

"I'm . . . I'm fine. Thanks for that coffee."

"Of course." His voice was deep and rough, and she imagined putting her cheek against his neck, hearing it rumble through his throat. "Hope your headache didn't last all day."

"Well . . . it did." She surprised herself with a giggle. "I never knew I was such a lightweight."

He chuckled too, and then said, "So. I'm just gonna dive in here." He coughed once. "I was hoping I could take you out for dinner. Maybe this weekend. We could meet somewhere if you like." When she didn't respond, he added quickly, "Or

I can pick you up, of course. I just wanted to mention it since we only just met."

"I don't know." Her body hummed, like electricity.

"I could wear a hat and you could throw it again, as many times as you like."

"Oh, about that. Sorry."

"You shouldn't be. I thought it was adorable." He paused. "Say you'll go out with me." He opened the request like setting up a tent on the grass, like a lovely possibility, and she realized she wanted to walk into it.

~~~

She'd been on pathetically few dates since the divorce.

Once, during her evening business course, a classmate—a paralegal in Baltimore's City Hall—had asked her to drinks after their midterm exam. He wore shirts so thin they revealed the outline of his white tank top. His ties were old-fashioned, wide and fat, his collars yellow and pilled. She'd looked forward all week to a nice glass of wine, but at the Charles Street bar, he casually said, "I'm just having a Coke. But get whatever you want, please." So she ordered a Diet Coke. And listened as he talked about himself—he was working this City Hall job, he was taking classes, he was stressed and lonely. Do you ever feel lonely? he'd asked. Like, you stay late at work just so you can be around other people? The next time he asked her out, she declined.

Back then, when she was in classes on a loan, working

part-time, she'd rented an apartment in Towson, within walking distance of the Light Rail—which she rode to campus—and the Valley Diner, where she waited tables on weekends and holidays. She volunteered for every holiday shift since she despised the hush that swept over the room whenever she entered her parents' house.

Every time she faced their front door, the pale wood with the plaque that read "God Bless This Home," she trembled, awaiting the hostility, but more so the smaller, more hurtful things.

Yes, she'd wanted to tell her classmate, while sipping a watery Diet Coke that night. I do feel lonely, all the time.

Once when she'd arrived at Ruba's house for Easter dinner, nobody had answered. Like a sad fool, holding a day-old pie from the diner, she tried all their cell phones. No answers, and she finally understood that they did not mean for her to attend. Baba had called her around 6 p.m. from the house phone—he'd never had a cell—to ask why she wasn't there yet. They'd decided to move their dinner to her brother's house because his yard was bigger, more suited to an egg hunt. She could tell Baba had not been part of the secret, and her heart swelled with love for him, for wondering where she was and calling her. "I'm stuck at work," she lied so she wouldn't upset him.

"You work too much, ya habibti."

"It's okay, Baba. I'll be graduating soon. It'll be better then."

She'd taken the Light Rail back to the apartment and given the pie to the homeless veteran who slept at the station.

And stayed home, in her cramped apartment, studying for midterms. It had been quite a lesson—hurt could be neutralized with focus, with determination. Eyes on the prize, she reminded herself that night. One day, they will know what they have done to you.

~~~

Samira laughed when she saw a Ford 150 pickup pulling into her driveway. Somehow in her mind, she'd stupidly imagined Logan would drive her to the restaurant in the Party Supply van.

"What's so funny?" he asked, standing in her doorway, looking delicious in dark jeans and a black corduroy sports jacket. His eyes brightened when she told him. "I should have done that. Woulda shocked the hell out of the valet."

It was an Italian restaurant in downtown Bethesda. The elegant bathroom had thick paper towels. Years ago, she would have squirreled several of them into her purse, she thought. Back at the table, Logan had ordered a good white wine and bruschetta as an appetizer.

They talked about work. "The party rental isn't my only business," he said. "I do landscaping when business is slow. But honestly, I prefer the party supply stuff more."

"Unloading chairs and setting up tents?"

"Yeah." He shrugged. "We never had parties as a kid. My dad wasn't good to my mom. Drank away our money. I like being part of other people's celebrations, I guess. That's probably weird."

"Sounds fine to me."

He asked about her, and she told him the minimum: Divorced. No kids. Recently promoted partner at a law firm specializing in education advocacy.

"Where's your office? Downtown?"

"In the high-rise by the harbor. Thirteenth floor."

"That's not lucky."

"Has been for me."

"You work in Baltimore but live all the way here in Bethesda?"

"I like the distance." Without thinking, she pulled a bruschetta off the plate and held it to his lips.

He didn't even hesitate. Instead he leaned forward, his eyes locked on hers, and devoured it in one bite. His lips brushed her fingertips.

"You're gorgeous. Is it too early to say this to you?"

"No." How glorious it felt.

"I'm divorced too," he said in the hazy, content silence.

"I'm sorry."

"I'm not." He shrugged. "She drove me crazy, left me pretty messed up. But I have a son. Caleb—he's twenty-six. My buddy. So not a total loss."

As their food arrived, she felt herself sliding into a darkness. If her body had not failed her, she thought, if it had done what it was designed to do, she could have had a child too. A buddy. She could have viewed being divorced the way he did—with a shrug and the satisfied feeling that it hadn't been a complete waste.

She held out her glass for more wine, feeling irritated. He poured her half a glass. "You can fill it," she told him.

"It'll be your third," he said gently. She gave him her best fuck-you look, and he smiled apologetically. "Just looking out for you," he said, complying.

"I'm forty."

"I'm fifty-two. But I can tell you don't drink too often."

"I can take care of myself."

He nodded acquiescently. "Understood."

They finished their meal, and when he suggested they go out for coffee to keep talking, she declined. Work, she explained. Later, at her front door, he put his hand gently under her chin. "This okay?" he whispered, leaning down.

Her irritation vanished. She nodded and the kiss rested lightly on her lips. But he pulled back just when she would have invited him to go further. Instead, he wrapped his arms around her and hugged her tightly. His beard brushed her forehead.

"I messed up tonight, somewhere."

"No."

"I did," he insisted. "I'd like another chance. Maybe next weekend? I'll even bring the box van if you want."

When she said okay, he kissed her lips again, then her temple, took her keys, and unlocked her front door.

Feeling happy and light, she pulled on his hand. "Come

in," she said softly. She watched, like a bystander, as her palm reached out, touched his collarbone, and slid down to rest on his chest.

Looking down at her hand, Logan exhaled sharply. When he looked up, he shook his head. "You've had four glasses of wine."

"So?"

"So that's why I have to say no."

"No?" She paused, stunned. Her hand fell away. "Holy shit."

"I'll call you tomorrow."

"Holy *shit*." She slammed the door in his face and, in a last frustrated burst of anger, clicked off the porch light so that he'd be drenched in black.

Two weeks later, the family met to discuss Baba's care. At least, these days, they called her to let her know where to go. These days, she no longer brought an old pie—she brought her checkbook.

At Ruba's house, the driveway was occupied with Muneer's rusty Corolla and Ruba's old minivan. She parked her Audi on the street, in front of Ruba's tilted mailbox with the red flag snapped off.

Mama was there too. "He can't live here," Ruba was saying as she walked in. "We have no room."

Mama said, "And if he falls again, how can I lift him?"

"We have eight people in this house," Muneer said. "Jamal

sleeps on the couch as it is." He looked up at Samira, who'd paused in the doorway. "Here's the voice of reason."

Samira kissed him on the cheek and he muttered, "Talk some sense into them."

Samira bent to her mother, who pulled her scarf more closely around her face and fiddled with the crucifix around her neck. She didn't kiss her back, only held out her cheek.

Ruba put a cup of coffee in front of her. "Are you sick?"

"No. But thank you."

"You look sick. You're not still upset about Jerome's news, I hope?"

"Jesus, Ruba. I was not upset."

"Mama, doesn't she look sick?"

"I didn't notice."

They told her Baba, who was home with the nurse, had left the remote control for the satellite dish in the freezer, ruining it, and now the TV was stuck on al-Manar, the Hizbollah-owned channel. Mama couldn't watch her Turkish soap operas until the new remote she'd ordered arrived. He'd started hiding the mail. The day before, he'd thrown all his shoes in the trash, insisting that they didn't fit. And today he'd spent an hour digging a hole in the lawn because, he claimed, his wife had buried his naturalization certificate there, the one that read "Palestine" in "place of origin."

"Well, did you?" Samira quipped, and everyone glared at her. Even Muneer. She didn't care. She was only here because if they locked Baba up in a nursing home, she would be the one who paid for it, the way she paid for all their dreams and disappointments, the banished daughter welcomed home because, of all the children, she was the only one who drove a new car. Who shopped at Nordstrom. Who wore a Cartier watch. Who no longer clipped coupons because it made her cry. Who took an annual vacation. The only one who'd achieved the American Dream.

And she'd done it without them.

Despite them.

Her phone buzzed as Mama and Ruba talked about possible homes. It was Logan. Again.

Free tonight?

> Sorry. Busy.

Busy lady.

> Nothing personal.

Give me another chance.

She glanced up at a sudden silence. Ruba stared at her.

"You are thinner."

"Maybe."

"Mama, isn't she getting too thin?"

"I don't notice these things."

Samira smirked. Mama never noticed anything about her. "Look," she said, standing up and pushing away Ruba's weak coffee, "let me know when you pick a place. I'll pay my share, but I need a say in what happens."

"Your share?" Muneer looked queasy.

"You can be made a guardian. I don't care," Mama muttered.

"It's called power of attorney."

"And with what money? A share?" Muneer said again. "Where do we find money for our share? Where would your mother find money?"

"Maybe start digging in the lawn." Samira headed to the door. "Who knows what else she's buried there."

~~~

Logan texted her again a few days later. She fired back quickly that it was a busier day than usual. That afternoon, she'd written up Rebecca for insubordination; Maysoon had discovered that she'd been emailing the client, negotiating a pushback of the deadline, without Samira's approval.

I'm staying home tonight. I'm done, she texted.

With?

The world.

Not me, though? Right?
RIGHT?

No. Not you.

He'd done the right thing, she'd had to admit. The gentlemanly thing. She knew that. But the rejection had clung to her like a wet blouse.

The worst part of her day came at 3 p.m. Ruba texted that

Baba had broken a window. The house was, he'd imagined, on fire and he'd been trying to escape.

It's time, Ruba texted. **Grand Oaks has a space.**

As she drove home, watching the clouds darken the sky, she realized that she would be losing Baba not once, not twice, but three times. The first was when Mama had kicked her out, with her arm still broken. He'd not been able to reach her. The second time was now, when he sometimes struggled to find her name.

And the third time was coming.

She turned on her street and realized she couldn't pull into her driveway. A large vehicle was blocking it.

Logan's box van.

She parked on the street instead, spying the lights in her garden, and opened the back gate. In the center of her walled garden stood a small, round tent, with long flaps down the sides. White lights were strung along the inside, making the opening glow. She entered and saw Logan standing beside a table, covered with a white cloth, and two chairs. A candle was nestled in a silver holder in the table's center.

He ushered her into a chair and pulled food from a cooler—plates of chicken, roasted potatoes, salad. "I thought maybe you could tell me about this terrible day. That made you done with the world. Except for me," he teased.

She stared at him, still feeling stunned. "This is the kind of thing guys do in those Hallmark movies. Guys named Blake or Maxwell."

He laughed. "This is also the kind of thing guys do when

they're crazy about someone. And when they happen to have access to a tent." He put a plate before her. "Come on. Tell me what happened today."

She told him about Rebecca's deceit, and added, "Plus my father is not doing well, healthwise." She regretted it when he asked for more details. "Oh, I'd rather not. I'll get upset." She diverted the subject. "How are things with you?"

"Well, I've spent a few weeks pursuing a very elusive lady," he said in his rumbling voice. Again she felt that wild impulse to lay her cheek against his throat.

She relaxed as they ate and chatted. He described a funny episode about a panicked family who ordered a hundred chairs but had fifty additional people unexpectedly show up. Samira laughed, but as she drew a breath again, something strange burst inside her. She gasped, clutching her napkin.

"Hey now . . ."

"Sorry—" She swallowed the next words.

"It's okay."

"My father—" She stopped as a tear slipped down her cheek, as her heart rate sped up, furious at losing control.

"Is he—"

"Not yet. But soon."

In a minute, he moved his chair beside hers and gripped her hand. It was strange, how quiet he remained, not asking any questions. There was such softness between them, and he kept murmuring, "I wish you didn't have to go through this," and playing with her hair. She imagined that, surrounded by the white of the tent, she was sitting in a cloud, that everything around her was constructed of light and emotion. There was nothing hostile, nothing angry, in this beautiful place he'd created.

After a time, she took him inside, through the front door, right to her bedroom. He started to say something, but she covered his mouth with her hand. "Logan, don't say no."

"But, honey—"

"Please. Don't say no."

He undressed her slowly, then himself. He watched her face intently as he made love to her, speeding up whenever she moaned, whispering in her ear, "God, I just could not get you out of my head, you know that? You got under my skin, woman." She lay in his arms later, because he'd asked to stay, and so she took the opportunity to place her head where she'd wanted, right up under his chin.

He chuckled, and his entire chest vibrated. "You're the best person to cuddle with, I swear."

"Thank you."

"For?" he prodded.

"The compliment. The nice dinner."

"And?"

"The tent was nice too."

"How about for the sex? And don't say it was *nice*."

They both laughed, but then his voice dropped. "Wanna talk? About your dad?"

"No. I'm good right now." She closed her eyes. "And tired, thanks to you."

He adjusted her so he could cradle her head in his elbow. "Then sleep."

~~~

Baba was quiet in the car, and at Grand Oaks, he looked around his new room curiously. He didn't know, Samira realized angrily. He had no clue.

"May I have a seat?" he asked the nurse in his accented English, as if he were visiting her home. "This lady seems poor," he told Samira in Arabic. "Her apartment is so small."

"Baba—"

"But it's clean. I like that. We were poor, too, but always, always, we were clean."

"Baba, you're going to live here for a while. We picked this place for you."

He ignored her.

An hour later, they tried to leave and when the nurse told him, "You're staying here, Mr. Awadah," he peered at her as if he were indulging a lunatic. Then his eyes rounded as she, Ruba, and Mama all headed out the door and waved goodbye. "No!" he yelled. "No! No!" he said again, his voice panicked.

"It's best to leave quickly," the nurse advised calmly.

"No! Don't go!" he continued to yell, as the nurse's tall body blocked the doorway. Mama turned and left, then Ruba.

Samira moved towards the door. He called her name feebly.

"It's okay," the nurse soothed her. "A clean break helps them adjust quickly. You can visit in a few days."

"Samira won't leave me," he snapped at the nurse in Arabic.

The nurse looked at Samira pointedly.

Samira left.

In the hallway, with her mother and sister, she listened to his outraged weeping.

"You said you'd tell him what was happening," Samira scolded them.

"He understands nothing. This morning, he chased the mailman because he thought he was going to rob our house," her mother answered.

In the parking lot, she watched them both drive away, but she couldn't turn her car on.

Samira won't leave me.

She called Logan.

"We took my father to a home today," she blurted out.

"I'm sorry, honey," he said. She could hear clanking noises behind, men talking loudly.

"Shit. You're working. I'm sorry."

"I'm fine. Hold on." A second later, he returned. "I'm in the cab now. Nobody will bug me."

"I shouldn't bother you." How shattered she must always seem to him.

"I'm the boss. I do what I want. And now I want to talk to you."

"He has dementia. He couldn't live at home anymore. I've known for months it was going to come to this." She told him she was still in the parking lot, sitting like a hostage. "The nurse said it was better to go."

"But that doesn't feel good to you."

"No."

"I always say go with your instinct, honey."

"But the nurse—"

"Is doing her job. I'm sure she's a nice lady. But that don't make it the best advice for you."

The nurse looked surprised to see Samira reenter the lobby, but she shrugged. "I know it's hard," and she patted Samira's hand. "Go on up now."

In his room, he sat on the couch, his hands on his lap. Someone had put the TV on the HGTV channel, some show about restoring an old house, but he wasn't watching it. Instead, he was clutching his masbaha and rocking back and forth, worrying the beads with trembling fingers.

She sat beside him, rubbing his back, calming him like a mother soothing an infant. An hour later, when he started to doze, she guided him gently to the bed.

As she bent to remove his shoes, he murmured in Arabic, "You left."

"I'm sorry. But I came back."

"And you made her leave."

She stayed quiet, holding one shoe in her hand.

"She couldn't stay, you said. She was too embarrassing."

He thought she was her mother, Samira realized. As she pondered how to respond, he suddenly screamed, "You bitch!"

He swiftly removed his other shoe and slammed it against the side of her head. Stunned, she reacted as she often had with Jerome, scuttling backwards like a crab. Not far enough. He whipped the masbaha across her cheek, then grabbed the other shoe and threw it against the wall, knocking down a lamp in flight.

She screamed.

The door opened, and four people in scrubs streamed in.

Samira watched in shock as one large man grabbed Baba's arms, clamping them to his sides. The nurse injected something into his arm while he struggled, but within moments, he wilted like a thirsty flower.

Samira returned home at 10 p.m. and recharged her phone, which had died. A text from Logan popped up.

How did it go?

I'm glad I went back.

When she saw him two days later, his eyes widened in alarm at the bruise on her face, but she swiftly, for reasons she didn't understand, lied. She'd tripped and hit her head on the doorframe. She didn't want him to judge Baba somehow, the way everyone else had, as if his actions explained anything at all about him. He'd hit her, yes, but he'd also revealed a truth that, after so long, was a balm to her busted heart.

One night, when she and Logan stayed up late talking, she described Mama's coldness, Ruba's greediness, Baba's swift decline. She told him a little of it. Not all.

Logan asked, "What did he mean that first day by 'You made her leave'?"

"My mother didn't want me home after my divorce."

"Why not?"

She shrugged.

"You don't want to talk about it. Got it."

"I'm sorry."

"Don't be." He told her she was like a locked box, filled with secrets. "Not pushing, but—I'd like to get closer. If you want me to. I'm ready."

"I just don't like to remember some things. That's all."

"Understood. I got some secrets too."

"Like what?"

"Like . . . I saw you dancing at that party, you know. At your sister's house."

She turned in his arms and stared at him.

"Yep. I'd come back to bring more chairs. And there you were, in the center, and well. Yeah. Damn, woman." He pointedly moved his gaze down to her hips and she cracked up laughing, and it didn't even feel strange anymore.

~~~

The nurse and staff all nodded when they saw her. They approved of her, she knew, and not because they knew she paid the astounding bill every month. They pegged her as a "good daughter," one who actually showed up several times a week. She'd seen the staff playing checkers, sitting for tea, watching TV with residents in the main hall. Trying to fill the void of being forgotten. How sad, she thought, to devote your life to your family, only to be shut away once you'd become inconvenient.

She entered his room and saw him at his kitchen table, muttering to himself.

She recalled the disastrous date she'd once been on, when she'd been asked, "Don't you ever get lonely?"

Backing out into the hallway again, she texted Logan on a whim.

Want to come over to meet my dad before our dinner tonight?

> **I can get there by 6.**
> **That okay?**

Perfect.

When he came, an hour later, Baba was good at first. Shook Logan's hand and invited him to have a seat. "Boil some tea for our friend," he told Samira grandly, like a generous host. Then he started to inquire about Logan's mother's health, and she knew they were losing him. But Logan played along, giving answers as best as he could, never once letting on that the situation was not quite right.

As they sipped tea, she whispered to Logan, "We can leave soon."

"I'm okay. Don't rush on my account."

She felt a small burst of gratitude in her heart.

"And how's your work?" Baba asked Logan in Arabic, and Samira translated.

"Good, good," Logan said, nodding amiably.

"And your brother and his wife? How are they?" Baba asked once again in Arabic, his voice growing suddenly cold.

Panicked, Samira picked up the teacups and carried them to the sink. "We should go," she told Logan.

"What's he saying?"

"He thinks you're my ex."

"Are you proud of how you treated Samira?" Baba continued, his voice shaking with rage. "Would you let your brother treat his wife like that? Eh?"

Samira grabbed her purse and signaled to Logan, who stood warily, watching Baba's movements.

"And she became like a leper, and all the blame fell on her head. You son of a whore!" Baba stood too. "You broke her arm, you animal."

Samira moved towards him, to settle him back in his chair, but he turned and picked up the clock on the side table.

Logan grabbed it first. He held both of Baba's wrists in one hand, the clock in the other. "Call someone," he told her grimly, shifting his legs to avoid Baba's kicks.

Back at Logan's house, an hour later, while he held her, she didn't mention Baba had hit her before. Several times.

She'd never told anyone, not even the nurse. If she did, they'd keep him sedated all the time.

She didn't want him that way. She wanted him to herself for a little while longer.

Because before his frenzied outbursts, his screaming rages, there were moments of lucidity. Of beauty and clarity. A few minutes at least during which he shone through, when he turned to her fondly and said, "Remember when I taught you to play tawla? And then you started cheating, you scamp." Those times—when he knew her, before the fog descended and obstructed his memory—those were worth it. During his good moments, when he called her "ya binti," she recaptured him. The way he loved her. She recaptured the way she used to love herself.

~~~~

When the doctor called her to confirm the news, she left work for the day. She didn't want to go home, didn't want to sit in the walled garden, not today, when she felt like soaring. So she drove to see Baba.

Ruba was there, with Mama. On his chair, Baba sat silently, empty-handed.

She looked through his cabinets, opened his refrigerator.

"What are you doing?" Mama snapped.

"Nothing. Nothing." But then she found his masbaha, buried in his utensil drawer. She walked over and handed the rosary gently to him. He looked at her in confusion.

"Hello, Baba. Salamtak."

"Hello, miss."

She patted his hand. "Here. Take this."

"Tell me," he asked curiously, his hand curling around the bright beads, "what should I do with these lovely things?"

Her heart squeezed. Even this?

"You're still losing weight," Ruba complained.

Baba's hands worked more frantically over his beads.

"We got invited to Lena's baby shower," Ruba added.

"You're going?"

"What excuse can I give?"

"For going to my ex-husband's third wife's baby shower? Oh, I don't know. Maybe that he treated me like crap?"

"He was in his rights to divorce you," Mama interjected wearily. "You have to accept that someday."

"Was he within his rights to break my arm?"

"You know what?" Ruba jumped back in. "Everyone feels sorry for you, okay? Every time I got pregnant, Baba would tell me not to talk around you. I had to hide my excitement so you didn't get upset."

"You poor darling . . ."

"There you go. With the sarcasm. And honestly, you should have offered to leave. A man has a right to want children."

"Well, I wanted them too. Maybe he had the problem, not me."

"Come on, Samira."

"I'm serious. It's so obvious."

"You shouldn't talk like that about a man," Mama cut in again.

"It's true—his second wife never got pregnant. And Lena's been married to him for years. Maybe he finally got some pills or something."

Mama and Ruba looked at each other and rolled their eyes.

That action caused her to speak it, to unfurl her lovely secret like a ribbon.

"I'm pregnant."

The words burst out of her mouth like dandelion seeds being puffed off a stem, gauzy and fragile, floating on an air current. They settled on Baba's standard-issue coffee table, between herself on one side and Ruba and Mama on the other.

"You're kidding." Ruba.

"Six weeks."

"Who?" Her mother.

"Nobody you know."

Silence. And then Mama stood up, reached across the table, and slapped her.

That's when Baba exploded.

Logan came to the hospital, where they'd taken Baba.

And that's where she told him, right in the hallway. Behind them, in the room, the doctors treated Baba for a suspected stroke after he'd raged in defense of Samira, then seized up and crumpled to the floor.

"Are you sure?" Logan asked her, gripping her by the shoulders. "I mean, you saw a doctor?"

"I did. Yesterday. He called me today and confirmed it."

"Why didn't you say anything before? When you suspected it?"

"I . . . I thought my cycle was just off for some reason. You have to understand. I've never been able to get pregnant before."

His hands rose to palm his cheeks, and his eyes looked dazed.

"This is a terrible place to tell you. And I don't expect anything from you. Honestly."

"You will marry me, woman."

"Logan!"

"Yes."

She shook her head. "I can't think right now. Not when my father is lying in there."

He nodded, took her hand, and led her back to the waiting room. They sat at one end, on a long couch. Across the room, near the Coke machine, sat her mother, sister, and brother-in-law, staring at Logan like a snake had slithered into the room. He lounged back on the couch, refused to look at them, but held fast to her hand.

Baba's stroke had been minor, but the CT scans showed bleeding in the brain. At midnight, the nurses advised them to go home, because he was not likely to wake up anytime soon.

Baba did not wake up the next day, or even the next week.

Except for attending weekly doctor's appointments—she was forty and considered high risk—she focused mostly on Baba. After a month, she agreed with the doctor that he should be moved to hospice. It was a matter of weeks, maybe days. Ruba disagreed, but Samira had the power of attorney now. Mama refused to speak to her.

Visiting him in the hospice one afternoon, she saw a family quietly exiting another patient's room. They all looked crestfallen, and she wondered if they'd just said their goodbyes. One of the men held a tiny infant, a newborn, in his arms.

It struck her then, as she sat by Baba's bed, watching his chest tremble as it rose and fell, that her baby would never know him as a grandfather.

Even of something as simple as this, she would be robbed.

Baba lingered, growing more frail every day. "It could be anytime," the hospice nurse said. "He's not awake, but you should feel free to talk to him. He can hear you."

She sat, fingering his worry beads, and told him about the baby, how she was terrified but also delighted. How she wouldn't let anyone ruin that for her. Not now.

Logan came to all her appointments, and during one, the doctor held a stethoscope to her still-flat belly. "Oh, we might hear the heartbeat," Logan said excitedly. Of course, she realized, he knew the drill. This wasn't his first baby.

But it was hers. And if she had to be honest, she was allowing herself to become more and more excited. More happy.

Logan still talked about marrying. "You just don't want

my box van parked in front of your fancy house," he joked, but he didn't push. Now, with the baby, with Baba fading, with ever-present work stress, now was a time to lie on the weak surface of water, to trust that its fragility could nevertheless keep her afloat. It could even, despite its transparency, carry her great distances.

One afternoon, as she and Logan stood together, browsing the bookstore for baby books, she observed him. How beautiful to be having not just a baby, but Logan's baby, she thought as she watched him leaf through a book, pause on a page, and shake his head in wonder.

Escorting the Body

Marcus Salameh

Baba died on a Tuesday, but Marcus knew nothing until Thursday. It had been five years, of course, but the neighbors remembered that the cranky old man with the accent had a cop son, so they left a message with the precinct: "Your father hasn't come out of his house in a couple of days. The newspapers are piled up on the lawn."

Marcus's old house key no longer worked. When Baba had told him, "I'm finished with you and your sister," he must have meant it. So Marcus gave the front door one swift kick, pounding it with his boot, and the hinges screeched, loosening their grip on the frame. The second kick brought it down, and Marcus walked in like a conqueror.

Though the smell was faint, he registered it immediately but paused to survey the room first. A lonely umbrella stood tall in a bucket by the front door. Baba's brown cardigan draped over the armrest of the couch, which was covered with a bedsheet, as it had always been. Marcus continued walking through the dining room, seeing the single plate with a fork, the food swept off cleanly, probably with a slice of bread.

He found Baba lying on the kitchen floor, faceup, his arms stretched outward like he was floating on water. The green sheen of his skin and the odor told him that it had only been two or three days at most. Not much bloating yet. The joints were stiff like rocks. The examiner later confirmed the heart attack had killed him sometime around Tuesday morning. In the kitchen, Marcus found some dried clippings of peppermint leaves—blackened and shriveled—scattered on the counter. A cracked teacup in the sink. He'd been about to make his morning tea. "It happened fast," the examiner said soothingly. "I doubt he felt much pain." Marcus thanked him politely, wishing he hadn't already heard him say these exact words dozens of times to grieving family members.

But maybe, in Baba's case, it was true. The old man had always been pretty damn good at avoiding pain.

The first call was to Amal. "She's feeding the baby," Jahron told him. "Something wrong?" he asked, then sighed at the news. "I'm sorry, brother."

"I'm glad you answered. I'm not sure how to . . . you know, say it to her. I need to read her mood."

"I'll tell her if you want. In a few minutes, when the baby naps."

"Thanks, man."

"I got it. Don't worry."

Next was Auntie Nadya, whom he didn't speak to, not really. He got her voice mail. "Call me back, Auntie." He left the message in Arabic, almost laughing that someone he knew still used voice mail. "I'm afraid I have bad news." That should clue her in.

She called him back quickly. "Sorry, ya 'amti," Marcus said when he heard her voice on the other end of the phone, "but my father has given you his remaining years." Bad news sounded kinder, almost generous, in Arabic, as if the dead had decided to bestow a gift upon the living. It was also a sweet way of dodging the pain of saying, "My father has died. My father, who cut me out of his life, is dead."

He'd heard Arabs grieve before, but he'd forgotten the keening, the raspy sobs, the sayings. Allah yerhamo. May God have mercy on his soul. May God keep him in his grace. Mercy. Mercy. Mercy. Marcus really doubted that, once God met his father, he'd want to keep him at all.

But his aunt's husband, Uncle Walid, called him back an hour later. Marcus was surprised because Walid Ammar had not spoken to him since his son's wedding years before, when Marcus had knocked the old man down for disrespecting his sister.

"Marcus, listen, you cannot bury him here."

"Why not?" he asked suspiciously. "There's a plot next to my mother."

"No, listen. You have to take him home."

"He is home."

"No, ya Marcus. He has to be buried in Palestine. And *you* must take him there."

Baba had allegedly said these words during a card game at Aladdin's, where Mr. Naguib let them stay past closing hours as usual. In front of Walid and six other men, Baba had raised his glass of arak and declared, "When I die, make sure they bury me back home. In my parents' gravesite. This goddamn country ruined my life. It won't have me in death too."

Apparently, it's what Baba had always wanted.

Marcus fought it anyway.

"We promised him, Marcus. We swore it." Walid's voice was urgent, insistent.

"You were probably all drunk," Marcus reasoned, trying to keep his voice calm.

"We knew what we were doing. And we promised."

"Exactly. *You* promised him. So you take the body."

"You're his son, ya Marcus. Hadtha wajib."

My duty, my ass, he thought angrily. Of course, their asses weren't the ones doing the paperwork. Walid would go if only he could, but he suspected he had an aneurysm, not that the doctor had diagnosed it, but he could feel it forming because all his kids drove him crazy and crossing the ocean in an airplane was playing with fire.

"Hadtha wajib," he said again.

"How will I know what to do? I've never been to Palestine. Not once in my life."

"It's your homeland, Marcus." That was Auntie Nadya, who took a turn getting on the phone to admonish him.

"Yeah, that's a nice thought, except I don't know anything about getting there."

"We will call Rita," she said, as if it were an easy fix. When he asked who this Rita was, Auntie simply said, "She takes care of the family's house there. She will help you."

And so he began. Police reports were bad enough, but the paperwork to have a body shipped across the Atlantic stunned him. Dealing with the Israeli authorities was like dealing with an angry, suspicious girlfriend.

"Why do you want to bury him here?" asked the Israeli embassy.

He explained, and they continued to pester him. "But why? Isn't he an American citizen? Why here?"

"His whole family is buried there."

"Not his brother Suleiman. He died in 2014. He is not buried here. And his wife is not buried here." That nugget of information sufficiently creeped Marcus out. It was intended to, he suspected, like when they asked a suspect a question when they already had the answer. He patiently played along with the game, and they finally acquiesced, probably figuring that letting a dead Palestinian come home was better than a live one.

The Palestinian Authority was easier: when he assured them he'd pay the fees they exacted, they said, "Ahlan wa sahlan," and signed off.

Jahron asked Marcus not to press Amal too much. It had been two months, but you never recovered quickly from a C-section, especially when you weren't expecting it. "She'll help you when you come back, to clear out his house," his brother-in-law promised, which reminded Marcus that this too was on what he considered his wajib list: clear out the house, deal with the paperwork, sell it. "I can . . . you know, come on the trip with you," Jahron added. "If you need the backup."

Thank god his sister was married to Jahron, he thought, not for the first time. Giving up Baba hadn't been too high of a price to pay. "That means a lot, but they need you. And who knows what I'm gonna deal with when I get there."

He bought a round-trip ticket to Tel Aviv. His sergeant gave Marcus two weeks bereavement. "Sorry to hear that, man. Were you close?"

"Not really."

~~~

When Mama used to talk about growing up "back home," Marcus simply could not imagine it. In Mama's stories, she was always fetching water from the well. In front of their house, when he was a kid, Mama had splurged and bought a wooden well lawn ornament and stuck it right by the steps. She planted real flowers around it and inside the damn thing too. "Marcus, I remember living in my first apartment in America," she said, "right off Eastern Avenue. And I couldn't believe water just came right out of the tap. I filled jars and buckets and Tupperware with it, because I was so sure it would run out. But it just kept flowing."

Marcus realized then that, while some people talked about growing up poor, his parents had been a whole different level of poor. Barefoot poor. Starving poor. Babies dying from diarrhea poor, like Mama's little sister, Amal, who had died before she was a year old.

Sleep on rooftops in the summer poor. Go to mass at two different times so your siblings can share the good shoes poor. Boil weeds to make tea poor.

While waiting in Ben Gurion Airport, where he'd been told to sit in a special room, Marcus thought about Mama, who was buried in America. She would not spend the afterlife with Baba, who was lying, packed in ice, in storage.

As he sat, having pushed his chair back against the wall, Marcus watched everyone, especially the guards carrying assault rifles strapped across their shoulders. Kids, really. One guy had a fungus-like acne spread across his chin, and more across his cheeks like a crusty blush.

He asked once what the holdup was about, and he was told

to sit down again. He followed their rules. He understood this. They were trying to wear him down. To assert authority.

So he waited.

Mama, in her last days, had told him to buy her a plot, if he could afford it, on the east side of the cemetery so the sun would rise on her grave. And he'd done it for her. Being buried in America was itself not an issue for her. No, Mama had embraced American life, finding delight in small things, in everyday places. The Dollar Tree, where she could buy everything from gardening gloves to bags of beans. She bonded with their Puerto Rican, Irish, and Black neighbors over exchanging coupons. She splurged on her Elizabeth Taylor Passion perfumes from CVS, and her Wet-n-Wild 99-cent lipsticks. You can live well, in this country, if you don't set your hopes too high.

Baba, on the other hand. Well.

"Marcus Salameh?" the pimply guard called him over, flapping some papers in his face.

"That's me." He stood and walked over casually, carrying his suitcase.

"We haf a problem. You cannot bring your fahzir to Israel," the kid said, and Marcus could swear he was gloating. "You don't have za permission."

Marcus stared at him for a second. When the soldier had caught his eye, Marcus held his gaze. Then he smiled. "I have had all the paperwork filed and authorized."

"It's not authorized."

"You'll have to tell me exactly why. The funeral home

handled most of this, and I have a letter from them that everything is in order." He made a point of taking a photo of the letter before he handed it over.

"Sit down, please. I'll be back."

He recognized this tactic too. The woman Rita had given him her WhatsApp number, and he messaged her. "Still here at airport. There's a holdup."

"Of course," she tapped back. "Call me when you leave airport. It will take time."

They summoned him a few more times, only to tell him to wait again. Over and over. After four more hours, he insisted that he be able to check on the body, to make sure it was being kept cool. After ten hours, when he realized he would be there all night, in this damn plastic chair, he messaged Rita, "Still here," and shut down his phone to conserve the battery. A young woman showed him a Keurig and he drank black coffee all night, worried about falling asleep.

It wasn't until early the next morning when they cleared him and the body to enter Israel.

"We can stamp your papers now," the soldier said. He looked refreshed, awake, having recently shaved.

Marcus's face itched from not shaving. His back hurt from the hard plastic chair.

He took the paper from the guard without a word.

"Your sleep was probably not very comfortable," the kid added, smirking.

"I didn't sleep," Marcus replied calmly. "As you know."

"Not at all?" the kid persisted.

Marcus sighed. He had spent the night worried not about himself, but about Baba, about the body decomposing in a warm room. It had been six days since he died. Embalming could stave off the inevitable for only so long. He couldn't even open the casket to check because it had been sealed tight for the journey. The old man hadn't spoken to Marcus for five years, and yet strangely enough, what had kept Marcus awake was white-hot anger, fueled by two fears: that he'd be unable to fulfill this wajib, and that his miserable, broken father, who hadn't seen Palestine for fifty years, might literally crumble before finally returning.

The kid was still smirking at him, so Marcus stared him down. "I've stayed up for days without sleep. Your little welcome doesn't faze me." He watched as the soldier flushed and straightened, then gripped the handle of his gun, but the attempt at being a badass only made Marcus smile because he could see the lock was still on.

Before he left, he powered up his phone and messaged Rita. "I'll send the taxi driver now," she wrote. "Al hamdillah a-salamtak." *Thank God for your safe arrival.*

"Does he have the address?" Marcus typed out wearily.

"We have no addresses here," came the curt response. "I'll tell him to bring you to Dar Salameh."

Not many cabdrivers had permits to enter Israel, so Marcus had been informed he was lucky that Abu Sharif had both a permit and a truck big enough to fit the coffin. He was someone's son's friend and he was willing to wait at the necessary military checkpoints.

The first thing Abu Sharif, who had a thick, bull-like neck, told him at the airport was "Salamit rasak" for his father's death. The second thing he told him was that his Arabic was funny. "You talk like my grandfather," he chuckled.

"How?" Marcus's head hurt from being so tired.

"Some of your slang. It's older people's talk."

That made sense. He'd only spoken to his parents. His older relatives. He couldn't read a single word, even though he could scrawl out his name by memorizing the curves and the slopes, how to round out the last letter, *sin*, like a hug.

"Do you know Rita?" Marcus asked Abu Sharif.

"Everyone knows Rita, habibi."

"After you take me to the house, can you help me find her house? She's supposed to help me with the arrangements."

"She will find you. Rest your mind."

Marcus settled back and watched the green hills and brown roads swim by, succumbing briefly to his weariness. He startled awake, only to have Abu Sharif pat him on the shoulder and say soothingly in Arabic, "Sleep, brother. I know they gave you a hard time. Sleep. All is well."

She stood like a general at the entrance to the house, which looked, to his eyes, like a compound. He'd seen a single picture of this house, a framed black-and-white photo of Baba, as a grinning teen with Travolta hair, seated on a stone ledge, surrounded by his siblings and their mother.

Baba was lanky and tanned, in a worn-looking pale suit. His smile showed bright white teeth, though his thick brows hung over his eyes like a grudge.

And yet he'd been smiling, and Marcus had always understood that once upon a time, in a land far, far away, Baba had been happy.

Suddenly, as the truck crawled towards the slim young woman standing before the house, Marcus nearly imploded with rage for the way that Baba's life had been trifled with. How his dreams—because surely he'd had them—were wasted on rage triggered by minor things, like a loud game of Simon Says, a burned meal, an unexpected bill.

The grave beside his mother would be empty, he realized.

I will be buried there, he thought a second later. That spot will be mine. Like Baba, he had to make sure everyone knew that.

"Ya helah, Sitt Rita," Abu Sharif said, putting the truck in park while Marcus tried to rid his mind of such dark thoughts.

His hands were shaking. And not because he was tired. He focused on the woman, who stood tapping away on her cell phone.

She wore all black, and her long hair hung in a loose braid over her shoulder. Her eyes were wide and pretty, her face round and smooth. She was small. Besides noticing that she was lovely, he also noticed that she looked annoyed. Possibly angry. So much fury compacted in a petite frame.

"I'm Rita," she said in good English, looking up from her

phone as she stepped right up to the truck. "I've had to rearrange everything with the priest." Speaking through the driver's side window, she began to give Abu Sharif instructions for taking the body right to the church.

Marcus pulled out his wallet while they chatted.

"I only have American dollars," he told the driver in Arabic.

The man waved him away. "Don't think about it. This is a time of mourning."

"No," Marcus insisted, knowing the Arab way. "If you don't take it, I won't speak to you again. You'll make me angry. Now, are American dollars okay?"

"They're the best, goddamn them all." He shrugged. "But I really can't take them."

Marcus reached over and stuffed the bills in the man's shirt pocket. "Enough. Thank you, brother."

Abu Sharif grinned at Rita. "He's one hundred percent Arab. Did you know he speaks Arabic so well?"

"Honestly, no," she said in Arabic, looking at Marcus. "We've only been texting."

Abu Sharif chuckled. "She's always texting, this one. Or on her laptop."

She rolled her eyes at Abu Sharif. "Yallah, tell Father we need to start in two hours."

"What starts in two hours?" Marcus asked.

"The funeral." She peered up at him. "Isn't that what you're here for?"

"Isn't it tomorrow?"

"How? We have nowhere to store him," she explained with a sigh. "Get your bags. While you shower and change, I'll let the town know."

"Just like that?" He gaped at her. "Everyone will be ready in a couple of hours?"

She glared at him as she opened the front door of the house. "This is a small village. Four hundred people. We've been waiting all week for you."

"Are you going too, Sitt Rita?" Abu Sharif asked hesitantly, quietly.

She nodded and went inside without waiting for him.

~~~

The church looked ancient, like it had been built right into the hill. Inside it smelled musty but also emitted the sweetness of incense. Marcus shifted uncomfortably on the old wooden pews, tired but worried it would snap under his weight. He was six-two, taller than any man he'd met here today. And he knew these pews sure weren't used to occupants over 200 pounds.

Rita sat beside him. She'd changed out of her black pants and blouse and into an all-black dress. Her face was pale, no makeup, no jewelry. So severe. So pretty. Her brows over her dark eyes were striking. Symmetrical. Arriving at the church, she'd stayed by his side as the well-wishers had hugged him, welcomed him home. He felt, at some points, he would collapse from exhaustion, so he found himself relying on her. "Stay here," she'd said once, when the line had ended and he'd tried to enter. "Abu Khaldoun isn't here yet. He limps, so it takes him longer to walk." And he simply obeyed, like a new recruit with a commanding officer.

Who was she? he wondered again, stifling a yawn. Auntie Nadya had only said, "Rita takes care of the house." Was she a cousin? A neighbor?

The priest, whose gray beard flowed down over his long black robes, began the ceremony, swinging the thurible from its golden chains, three times, three times, releasing the incense in puffs of pale smoke. They sang songs over Baba's body, chanting in Arabic—Marcus did not know the words, but the chorus soothed him. The priest read passages from the Bible, then released more incense. Then more reading. And more incense.

"Marcus, I need to discuss something with you . . . a tricky matter, before people start coming to the house," Rita whispered to him.

"Who's coming?"

"That's what I wanted to talk about."

"The guests? Who's coming over?"

She looked up at his face calmly. "Everyone."

He turned and scanned the church, which was so full that men huddled around the side and back walls. The officer in him screamed that this was a fire hazard, with only one door, should one of these tapered candles tip over and light the tapestries. How could all these people fit in the house? He'd barely looked around earlier as she'd rushed him through.

Here's the bedroom. The hammam. The kitchen. Y'allah. Y'allah. The dead have waited long enough.

A few minutes later, Marcus was carrying his father out of the church, with the help of Abu Sharif and four others who stepped forward. The graveyard was on the outer edge of the church, a field of yellowed and soot-stained stones, carved in Arabic script.

"This is your father's tomb," one man said, pointing to the stone. "See? There's your name."

"He can't read Arabic," Abu Sharif told the men, then turned back to Marcus.

"This is your family's tomb. It's always been ready for your father," he answered, calling out to a man with a crowbar. There were no shovels. No grass to be unearthed. There was no dirt to be moved. Marcus watched as they pried the heavy stone lid off the large box, then he helped push it aside, sweating and panting, until a great cloud of dust emerged like wispy clouds of mortality. When there was enough space, they lowered the casket into the hole, while the priest chanted behind them and people made the sign of the cross. They restored the lid, and the priest splattered holy oil over the sealed tomb. One man bent down and scrawled in chalk, "Bashir al-Salameh, Abu Marcus."

"I'll have someone do the carving tomorrow," Rita assured him.

And then it was over.

His heart thumping, his head aching, Marcus felt satisfied. He'd returned Baba to Palestine in death, even if not in life.

"Allah yerhamo," people told him, solemnly shaking his hand as they filed out of the cemetery. "It's good that you brought him home," they said. Some people called him Abu Bashir—if he had been a truly dutiful son, that would indeed have been his name. But as he looked down upon the heavy stone tomb, he thought to himself, if he'd had his own boy, he never ever would have named that child after his angry, sad father.

He walked back to the house with Rita at his side, her head barely reaching his shoulder and her hair in a long braid down her back. Though she was small and quiet, he was intensely aware of her.

"So, who are you to my family?" It was blunt, but he hadn't slept in thirty-six hours and was about to face a house full of well-wishers for the rest of the day.

She looked up quickly, then straight ahead again. "I grew up here with your family. I've lived across the street my whole life."

"But you take care of the house for us?"

"Yes, ever since your aunt got married and moved to Nazareth."

"Why?" He wished he could cut off his interrogation side, his need to understand exactly the sequence of cause and effect. His training took over, his instinct to ask questions, to parse through alibis.

"Because if it remained abandoned, they would come and take it."

The settlers. He turned back and looked at the direction

from where they'd started, and he saw the large white homes on the hillside, flanked by watchtowers, bordered by security fences. A new city—a "settlement" made it sound like a damn campsite—built to replace this village. Settlers who wanted to push these people out, like pioneers pushing out Natives on the frontier.

"Is that okay with you?" she asked sarcastically as they approached the house.

He frowned at her, but she surprised him by laughing in response and opening the front door.

"The visitors will come in waves," she explained inside, motioning for him to line all the available chairs around the room. She pulled out a cell phone and called three neighbors, asking them to bring any chairs they could spare. "The man doesn't know how to prepare," he heard her tell someone. "I'll stay to help. Bring what you can."

Ten people showed up at first, and Rita did it all. Boiled coffee in a large pot on the stove. "Let me help you," he said, checking on her as she stirred the fine grounds in the water.

"No, no, they're here to talk to you," she said, waving him back to the living room.

The guests only stayed for twenty minutes each, all saying the same thing: Allah yerhamo. God have mercy on his soul. May his memory be eternal. The phrases rolled soothingly off their tongues, like the thurible being swung, filling the room with sweetness. Rita moved among the guests like a butterfly, hovering to light a cigarette, passing trays of coffee, offering napkins. She returned to the kitchen between waves to wash out the cups, start another pot. Only one person commented on her presence: "Rita is such a good girl, the poor dear."

They asked when he was leaving. He wasn't sure, but one old woman calmly informed him he'd stay until the one-week memorial mass. "Your wajib, habibi," she said as if it were the most indisputable thing in the world, as if his wajib weren't the only goddamn reason he was here, far away from Baltimore, from his beat, from his life. "I doubt it," he said, but the woman, Imm Moussa, patted his arm and said Rita would handle it all. "And you come and visit me soon, okay?" she asked, though it was clearly a command.

"He will," Rita told her, and he looked between these two tiny women—perhaps he was heavier than their combined weight—and wondered why on earth he was planning to obey them.

But he did indeed obey. One couple, who'd brought their twentysomething son, talked about how his wedding had been planned for so long, but of course, mourning assumed precedence. He was unsure why they kept repeating this fact until Rita pulled him into the kitchen; apparently, he had to grant them permission to not wait forty days. "Say something like good news should never be delayed, or whatever," she hissed. And he did. He said exactly that. In relief, they insisted he attend the wedding.

Three hours later, when the last wave had receded, long after darkness had fallen, he found her in the kitchen, her arms immersed in soapy water. When she saw him, she quickly turned and pulled down her sleeves, then rinsed the pot one final time.

He saw them anyway, the ropey scars on her forearms.

Rather than ask, he held up a pack of cigarettes. "I haven't smoked since high school. Twenty-five years ago."

"Are you sure you're even Arab?" she shot back, but she smiled and dried her hands.

"Is anyone waiting for you at home?"

"No." There was no feeling in this word, which burst out like a bullet.

"Let's sit on the balcony," he said. "I have six cigarettes in here. We can split them."

They sat in the cool blackness of the night, the balcony illuminated by the kitchen light coming from the window, and smoked quietly. Marcus was tired but his body was humming. After the second cigarette, she suggested more coffee. "It's late," he said, and she laughed at him and went to the kitchen anyway.

"Show me how to make it," he asked. He would be here, it seemed, for at least seven days, until the memorial. He would have to make it for himself every day. He couldn't remember the motions his mother used, even though he could easily picture her, as she usually was, at the stovetop, stirring the coffee. Now he watched and memorized Rita's instructions—three heaping spoonfuls for each small beaker of water.

"Do you use sugar?" she asked him.

"Not really," he said. "I prefer it without."

"Like me," she said. And she smiled at him, almost shyly. "I like it when it's bitter."

~~~~

Rita was always in motion. Either tapping away on her laptop, taking walks to talk to people in town, or speaking on the phone. She didn't have a job, she claimed, but seemed busier than everyone. She moved in ways that confused him, but that felt familiar. After all, he'd spent two decades watching his own sister be crushed.

Amal had been penned in half her life: no boyfriends, no dates, no sleepovers, no school functions until she imploded one day and started to attack herself, to carve up her own skin and sanity with drugs, boys. Mama had died by then, and Baba had lost all authority anyway. And so he'd resorted to silence. He cut her out, like throwing her memory into a stone vault, walking away, leaving it unmarked.

Rita didn't seem like a person who could ever be caged. Her body was lithe, confident. She wore tight jeans and black T-shirts, and her hair was always braided, simply, a shiny rope that trailed down over her shoulders or down her back, the tail tapping her ass as she walked.

Of course he noticed.

She told him that he had to repay some of the visits. He asked her to come with him.

"No."

"I know you have a life," he apologized. "But I need—"

"No," Rita repeated, before leaving to cross the road to her own home. "No, I really don't."

"I don't actually know much about her," he told Imm Moussa during his promised visit.

She pushed a cup of black tea towards him, then tapped her palm over her heart. "Ah, the girls suffered the most."

"What girls—"

"During the intifada. We don't talk about it. The boys with the stones, yes, we talk about them. But not the girls." She assured him that Rita stayed busy on her laptop and in her community service and hamdillah for her sanity. Then she returned the conversation to Ibn Hanna's wedding, which was coming up, and to life in America, and how had his people really elected that terrible casino owner as president. Didn't Americans know gambling was haram?

~~~~

Ibn Hanna's wedding was on Saturday, a few days before the one-week memorial. Marcus spent the day being lazy, sleeping until almost noon, then making a small pot of coffee and downing it all. He'd messaged Amal in Baltimore to tell her he'd be gone for a few more days because of the memorial. And more paperwork, because apparently, there was an inheritance. A piece of land that could be sold; according to the law, one full share went to Marcus, the son. Half a share to Amal, the daughter.

"That's fucked up," Amal said.

"I'm not going to do that, obviously," Marcus said. "It'll be fifty-fifty. What do you think?"

"I don't want shit from him," she said flatly.

Marcus explained to Rita, who was helping him with the legal issues, that Amal wouldn't be claiming her share. When she asked why not, he said simply: "She and my father didn't talk."

"Haram. She didn't talk to her own father?" He avoided the answer, but she pressed him several times, seeming genuinely surprised. "What kind of a girl doesn't talk to her father?"

"Excuse me," he snapped. "*He* didn't talk to *her*, and don't pass judgment on my sister." She didn't respond, just watched him quietly, until he sighed and added, "Anyway, I'll use her half to start a fund for my nephew. I'll have to call my bank."

She nodded. "That would work."

"You approve, inshallah?" he teased, trying to restore the light mood. She was so damn somber.

"I do. I don't understand, though, how a father and daughter do not speak to each other." Back to that.

He hadn't answered. That was yesterday, he thought now, drinking his coffee on the balcony. Tonight was the wedding. Tomorrow, more visits. He apparently had to visit the priest and make a generous contribution to the church. Tuesday was the memorial. Wednesday, Abu Sharif would come and drive him back to Tel Aviv, where he would board a flight to Baltimore. To home. To desk duty, to training academy, to homicide work. Back to working showers and regular, dependable water flow and Wi-Fi.

But for now, there was a wedding.

He was invited to stroll through the streets, clapping and singing as the groom's family walked to the bride's house to escort her to the church. The walk to the church was equally festive, and Marcus was carried away by the clapping, the ululations, the sheer exhilaration and joy and love that filled the air. He found himself smiling, and understanding for the first time why Baba had always wished to return.

"It's nice to have you home," Imm Moussa told him at the reception in the church hall, where they served trays of peanuts and simple sandwiches. She said this as if he'd been away for a vacation, not absent his whole life.

"I don't know why Rita is not here." He paused deliberately. His favorite interrogation trick. It always worked.

"Rita doesn't come to these events."

"Does she get invited?"

"Sometimes. But she never comes," she repeated. "It's been that way since she was released."

"From?"

"Oh, if you don't know, then maybe I shouldn't say."

He smiled and tried a new tactic. "No. It's okay. If she has a bad reputation, then maybe I shouldn't be spending so much time with her. I appreciate that you—"

"She is the best person, with the best reputation, more pure than Maryam, the mother of Jesus, in fact." Imm

Moussa was outraged, the skin under her chin trembling with fury.

"If you say so, ya Auntie."

"What happened is not her fault." She shook her head. "That's what they did to punish the girls' brothers. To keep their fathers and uncles off the streets."

Marcus tightened his grip on his glass, feeling sick to his stomach. "When was she released?"

"After the baby died."

~~~

He left soon after that, after leaving an envelope with two crisp hundred-dollar bills with the groom. He'd never been inside her home but he knew which door was hers. He knocked firmly, because her neighbors on either side were at the wedding, spiraling in the dabke line, dancing and singing.

She peeked through the window, and he saw her hair was down around her shoulders and hips. Her dress was an old thobe which seemed worn and soft, so maybe was used as a nightgown. "What are you doing?" she asked, pulling open the heavy metal door.

"You're awake."

"I don't sleep."

"I need to talk to you."

"About what?"

"About you."

She came out on the marble step, then looked around. The alley was quiet. In the distance, they heard the music and the drums from the church hall.

"Why are you home?"

"I don't go to parties."

"Why not?"

"None of your business."

"Do they make you feel bad?"

"Marcus, I don't owe you an explanation of my life," she said, turning and heading back inside. She tried to shut the door behind her, but he was quick, his reflexes kicked in and he jammed his shoulders through the entrance. "Wallak . . ."

"Why were you sent to prison?"

"How dare you." She watched him, shocked, as he calmly walked into her living room. It was a simple room: on a small table sat her laptop, beside a figurine of some warrior goddess; there was tatreez on the wall; white curtains veiled the window.

He pulled a packet of cigarettes out of his suit jacket. "I have four. How many do you want?"

She walked over to a small closet and opened it. When she turned around, he saw an old wooden rifle in her hands, and it was pointed right at his head.

"Okay, okay," he said, and turned around. "I'll go." As he left, he looked at the inky sky and realized this was the second time in his life a woman he admired had aimed a gun at him.

The next morning, she walked into his kitchen, where he sat with his coffee as if nothing had happened. "Sabah al khayr," she said smugly as she poured herself some coffee.

"Sabah al nour." He eyed her warily. "Should I search you for weapons?"

"It wasn't loaded." She waved her hand dismissively.

"I know."

She turned to study his face. "How did you know?"

He shrugged. "I've handled every kind of weapon you can imagine."

"Oh, is that right?" She looked upset. Angry. "Then why did you leave?"

"Because I was scaring you."

She laughed loudly, clamping a palm to her heart. "Wallahi? I pointed a gun at you, but you were scaring me?"

He remained quiet. She stopped laughing and took a seat beside him at the table. They stayed that way, not saying a word. He felt that if he pursued this topic, if he scaled her carefully constructed wall of bravado, that she would walk out and he would not see her again. Or if he did, he would not see her, but a false Rita. A performing Rita.

They spent the day in Ramallah, filling out paperwork. He tried to call Amal again, but got the same answer: She wanted nothing from Baba. Nothing from his inheritance.

He talked to Jahron. "Listen, we get a piece of land here,

and there's a man who wants to buy it. It's going to sell for a lot, man. Just take it and put it away for the baby."

"I'm going to do what your sister wants, man. This is not about me."

"It's not about money. I can transfer it to you."

"Right, so she never trusts me again? Come on, you know better than that."

He noticed Rita signing forms at the lawyer's office as well. "What's this for?"

"She gets a small amount as well, as left by your father."

Marcus was still puzzled. He wished he could read the forms. He had to trust what they were telling him, that Rita had been left 100,000 shekels in an addendum, made five years ago, in his father's will.

Rita picked up falafel sandwiches and they took a cab back to the village. Sitting on the balcony, quietly eating, watching the children play in the courtyard and listening to the church bells toll, Marcus felt oddly comforted. He felt sad for Amal, and even sad for his father. It didn't have to be this way. Baba could have been more loving, more caring, more generous with Amal, and she would have been here with him, mourning him. But it was hard to mourn someone you didn't understand, who locked himself away.

He watched Rita, carefully eating the last bites of her sandwich, a napkin spread on her lap, her hand lifting a glass to her lips. She sat on the edge of her chair—she always sat like this, as if she could more easily jump up and run—and the end of her braid rested in a small heap on the seat behind her.

"If you want to learn how to load and fire a gun, I can teach you."

She swallowed her last bite and carefully wiped her mouth with the napkin. Then she cleared her throat, staring at the crumpled napkin in her hand. Then she said, "Please."

They only had a couple of days. He advised her to find a real gun, something small she could hide and pull out more quickly, and she did. He didn't ask where or how, and all she offered was that Abu Sharif the truck driver was resourceful. The spot they found was on the outskirts of the village, on his father's land, where there were olive trees and fields of patchy dark grass. This was better than the other side, the west side of the village, because that was where the Israeli-only road ran and the settlers who used it were all armed. This side was quieter for now, because the olive harvest had already ended.

They used several cans as targets. Marcus showed her how to load the gun with the clip, and she became impatient. "We're not shooting anything until you can get this part down," he told her patiently. She rolled her eyes, and he burst into laughter. "You're like the new recruits we get—they all want to be hotshots before they know how to handle the equipment."

When she could do it smoothly, he lined up the cans and let her take aim. "Watch yourself on the kickback," he told her, "because you'll hurt your arm." Several times, he pushed her braid to the side and stood behind her, steadying her hand. "Line it up," he said softly. "Line it up. Now. That's it. Fire."

Several hours later, when the sun had risen high, centered in the noon sky above their heads, they found the shade of an olive tree and ate their lunch. "You hit the cans the last few rounds. I can move them farther back maybe. I don't think you'd ever have to fire from such a long range."

She was quiet and thoughtful. He liked how she could do that with him, just sit and not talk and the peaceful cloud continued to hover above them. She didn't talk just to fill the silence. She liked silence, he realized. So did he.

"They arrested me in 1989," she said. "I was fifteen."

"For?"

She blinked at him, her eyebrows rising. "For . . . throwing stones. For trying to get to school. For being Palestinian." She shook her head. "For every reason and for no reason. It was the intifada."

He was ashamed that he knew so little about it. Baba had never really explained politics, never talked about why he was shouting at the news, trembling over an Arabic newspaper.

"A lot of the girls who got arrested . . . we got hurt in jail. Not just beating us. More than that."

He knew that already, but hearing her say it . . . it still slammed into him. The thought of someone forcing her, her slim body, her slim arms.

"I was in there for eight months. I got out because I was part of the hunger strike. One of the hunger strikes."

She shifted until her back leaned against the tree, her fingers plucking at the tough, sparse grass. "When I came out, I was a hero for a month. Everyone came to my parents' to welcome me back. And I was so sick, I didn't notice at first. But soon, I started to see that I was like an infection. Nobody wanted to catch me."

"They stopped socializing with you."

"Not in a mean way. They always talk about me still like a hero. How brave I am. But nobody let their daughters hang out with me. Nobody wanted to marry me. When my parents died, I felt like, with them gone, I wouldn't have any connection to anyone. And it's true. Nobody comes to see me. One time, some guys from another village were here for a wedding, and they came around my house. I screamed and someone came and chased them off. But that still wasn't enough. And when people invite me places, I know they don't really want me to come. It's like they don't blame me for what happened, but they don't want me to be here either."

"I'm so sorry."

She pulled on her braid, sweeping her fingers along its length. "I had such a hard time finding work. Your father fixed that, of course."

Marcus stared at her. "Explain."

She looked back at him. "He was my employer."

"He paid you."

"Yes. To oversee the house and the land. To handle

the olive harvest every season. He sent me a check every month."

"For how long?"

"For the last . . ." She shrugged. "After my mother died. So, fifteen years it's been."

"I didn't know a thing about it."

He'd been very kind, she explained, seeming unsure now as she watched his expression. Marcus kept his expression neutral but inside he was roiling. "He called me when my father died, and he sent my mother a check at the time. But then when mama died too, he called me every month to see how I was. He sent me money every once in a while. But then, I still couldn't find a job, and your aunt moved to Nazareth, and he asked me to take care of the house."

Marcus suddenly couldn't hold himself upright any longer. He lay down on his back, on the dirt and the rough grass, his heart hammering. He took slow breaths—inhaling and exhaling, to a count of four each time, making a square—and tried to think. This girl had been rejected by everyone, but saved by his father?

"What are you thinking?"

"I'm thinking," he said, feeling the anger—there it was—surging into his throat, "that my father was a hell of a lot nicer to you than he was to me. And to my sister."

"He never really talked about your sister. He said it made him upset to think about."

"Upset? What the FUCK?" He immediately regretted his roar, because she scuttled back, away from him.

He reached out and grabbed her hand. "No, no. I'm sorry. Rita. Please."

"Don't yell."

"No, I won't." He sighed shakily. "Bastard."

"Don't call him that, Marcus."

"I don't know what else to call him. That's the kindest word I have right now."

The memorial was held in the afternoon on Wednesday. By then, he and Rita had been busy—he'd sold the parcel of land, had wired the money to himself in Baltimore. He'd set up a guardian account for his nephew and put a large chunk of the money there to let it grow. It would collect a small interest, and maybe he should look into investing it, he was told, but that would come later. Right now, he didn't want to gamble with one more thing.

Except Rita.

She said no at first. Because it was pathetic. Because it was false. It was practically fraud, she argued. And besides, she didn't need him. Or anyone.

But in the end, she'd been convinced. What choice did she have? People married for lots of reasons, and love wasn't usually one. Sometimes marriage was nothing more than the cool shade of a tree in a scorching desert you couldn't otherwise survive. That's what bothered her the most, she said. What? he asked. "That I don't really have another option," she replied.

And so, before the memorial service, the priest met them in his office, and they walked solemnly to the altar. He married them quietly, in front of the icon of the Virgin Mary and Joseph the carpenter. The truck driver was there to witness, as was Imm Moussa, who happened to be there to put fresh flowers at the altar.

"When will you join him in America?" she asked Rita, who wore a simple black dress, her hair down but gathered in a clip. Marcus had actually gone to Ramallah and bought a new suit—his third one, a rich navy blue—because this moment might not be magical, but he felt deeply that nothing that had happened in his life before this moment mattered.

They didn't answer, but they'd talked about it extensively. Rita would come only if she needed to. He would arrange her papers, and when she felt that it was really unbearable, she would use their marriage like a ticket to leave.

After the wedding, before the memorial, they had a few minutes alone in the priest's office.

"I want you to come, you know."

"This is still my home."

"You don't sleep at night."

"That's because of my memories, and they will follow me no matter where I live."

He lifted her hands and kissed them, then kissed her cheek. Then once, softly, on her lips. She stood still, regal, not moving.

"I'm sorry. I should have had a ring."

"No matter." She finally smiled. "You gave me a gun."

On the morning he left, he held her for a long time. She allowed him to. He rested his chin on her head, hugging her tightly. He understood she might never come. That this might be the last time he would see her. She might never, ever feel it was bad enough to board a flight and cross an ocean to start again. She might remain here, not living, just existing, in this village until she died.

One thing was certain, and he told her this too: He knew he, at least, was never coming back, unless he had to come, to "collect you, like a package, and bring you home," he promised. "I'd come then." And as the truck pulled away, he turned and watched her slim figure shrinking in the distance, standing in front of the house where he'd first seen her, and he thought his life was rewinding itself. Instead of getting closer, she was now shrinking in the distance until she was gone, and he thought, during his quick time at the airport, and on the whole flight, that she was the most heroic woman he'd ever met.

He told Amal about her. He told her the story of how their father had been someone else's savior this whole time. "It doesn't change how I feel," Amal said finally. "I'm moving on."

But how could he do that, Marcus wondered. How do you just bury a wish, a longing, the way he'd buried his father's body? The fact was this: Their father *had* been capable of compassion. Of defying society. Of making sure a vulnerable person was not thrown to the wolves. Just not with his own children.

He went back to work. He solved a big case in the city—a drug gang that was plaguing the west side. He arrested six men in one month on domestic violence charges. He outed a cop who'd been part of a laundering scheme. He showed up to hearings to testify. He trained recruits. He wrote reports. He kept people safe and then he went home to his quiet house and tried not to think about the emptiness, the stillness, that pervaded it. He slept with the TV on most nights, just so there would be some noise, the sound of people talking.

His nephew celebrated his first birthday. Amal was healthy and working part-time as a social worker, while Jahron was busy as a music teacher. He sent a picture of himself holding the baby to Rita on WhatsApp, and she replied, "Okbal al 100 sena." Such a lovely wish—a hundred years of life. The Arabs were a people that knew life could be horrifically unjust and unfair—and yet they cherished it. "Are you sleeping well?" he asked her, and she replied that her nights were still impossible. The holidays came and passed, and he attended the precinct's Thanksgiving dinners and Christmas parties, watching people pull each other under the mistletoe in the commissioner's doorway. He messaged Rita during these times, wishing her a merry Christmas; he'd mailed her a simple gold band as a Christmas gift, and she'd messaged him a thank-you. At the precinct party, he was surrounded by laughter, and he understood that these were people who saw so much ugliness that they reveled in these small moments. But he remained on the sidelines, watching their gaiety and feeling very much alone.

And then, one day a few months later, his phone rang. He answered and heard her soft voice again.

"Marcus, please. I'm ready."

"Yes," he replied. "I'll be there."

Acknowledgments

Thank you to the journals that first published the following stories:

"Ride Along," *Fifth Wednesday*, Fall 2017, Issue 21.

"Behind You Is the Sea," *The Michigan Quarterly Review*, Summer 2021.

"Mr. Salameh Gets Drunk at the Wedding," *Philadelphia Stories*, Winter 2022.

"Cleaning Lentils," *Kweli*, Summer 2022.

I am grateful for the support of the Robert W. Deutsch Foundation in the production of this work, specifically for awarding me a 2022 Ruby's Artistic Grant. Thank you to the Maryland State Arts Council for naming me its state-level winner of a 2022 Individual Artist Award.

~~~

I'd also like to thank many people in my life who offered me either support or a welcoming space to talk, experiment, and create: Celeste Doaks, Rosalia Scalia, David R. Marshall, Laura Pegram, Carla DuPree, susan abulhawa, Sahar Mustafah, and Eugenia Kim. Warmest thanks to Tom and Elaine Colchie, who have encouraged my growth as a writer for almost a decade; I am immensely grateful to you both. To Ryan Amato, Ashley Yepsen, Lucile Culver, Crissie Johnson Molina, John McGhee, Chloe Bollentin, Sierra Delk, Anna Brower, Yvonne Chan, and Terry McGrath for their help, guidance, and wisdom; your support of this novel has been invaluable. And to Stephen Brayda and Alicia Tatone, who captured the spirit of this work in its gorgeous cover—so many thanks! To Gabriella Page-Fort, thank you for sharing both my vision and my hopes for this novel—working with you is an honor and a gift.

And to my children, Mariam, George, and Gabriel, my joy, my reason for everything: the only time words fail me is when I am trying to describe how completely I love you.